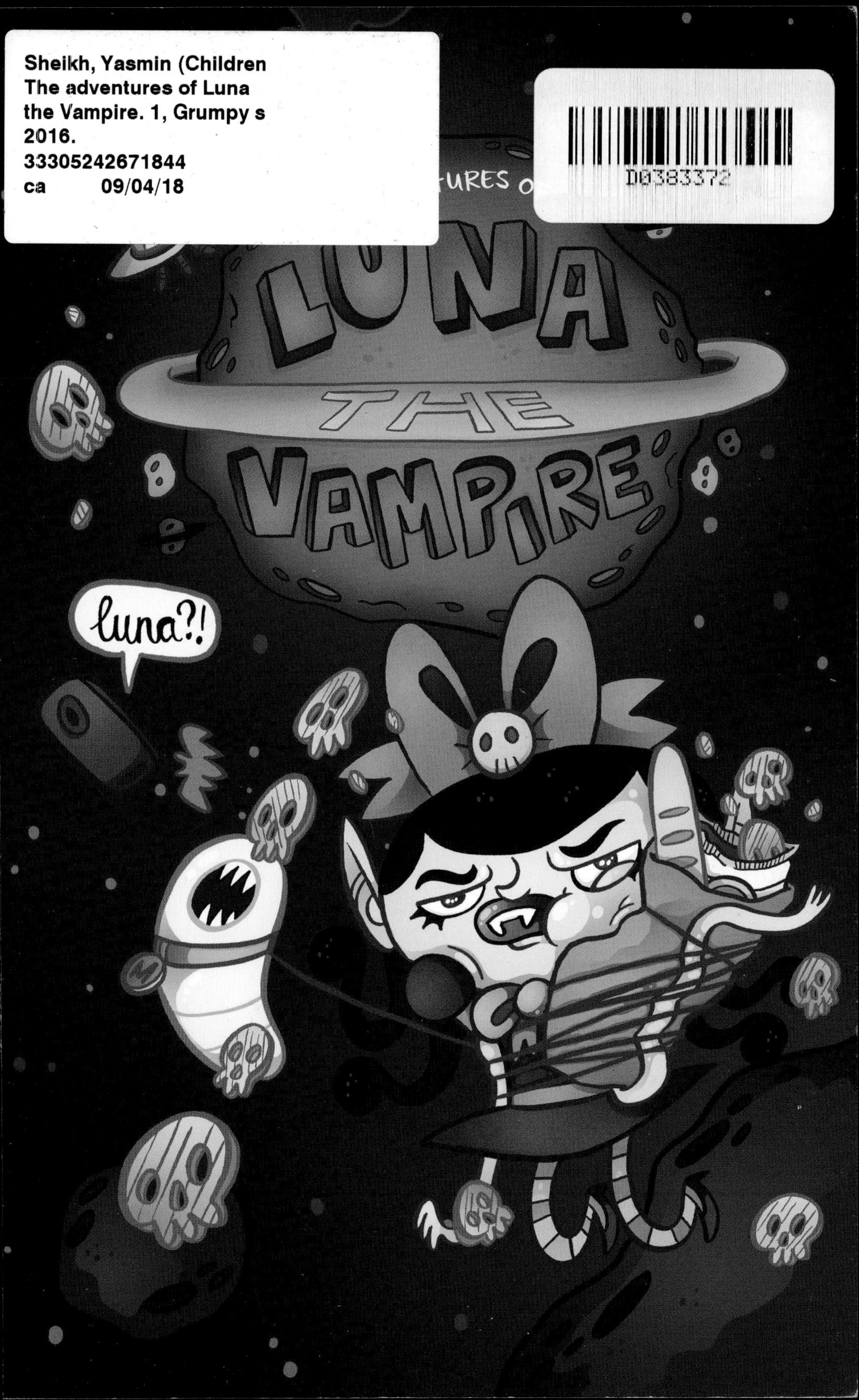
...URES O...
LUNA
THE
VAMPIRE
luna?!

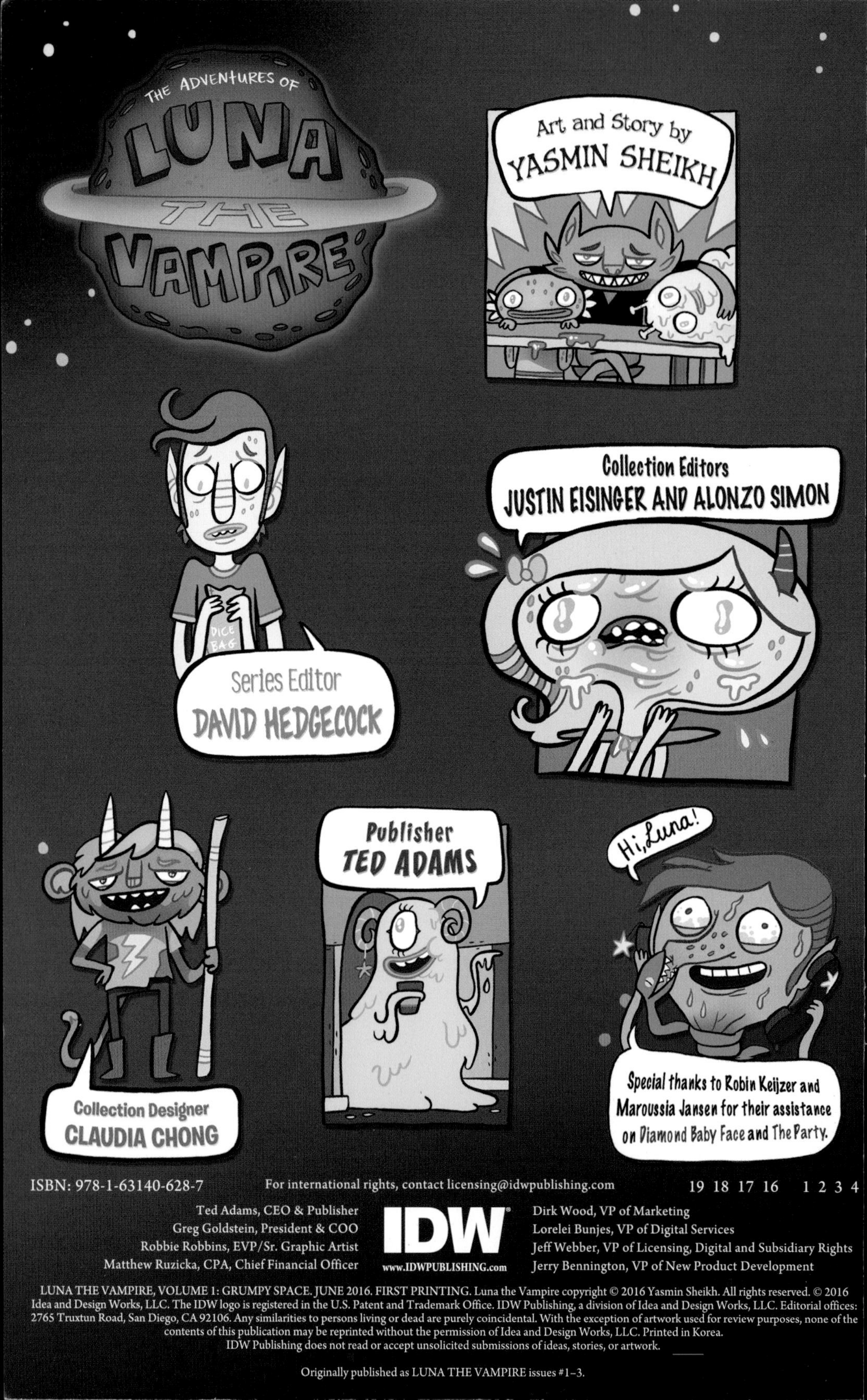
THE ADVENTURES OF
LUNA THE VAMPIRE
Art and Story by
YASMIN SHEIKH
Collection Editors
JUSTIN EISINGER AND ALONZO SIMON
DICE BAG
Series Editor
DAVID HEDGECOCK
Publisher
TED ADAMS
Hi, Luna!
Collection Designer
CLAUDIA CHONG
Special thanks to Robin Keijzer and Maroussia Jansen for their assistance on Diamond Baby Face and The Party.

ISBN: 978-1-63140-628-7

For international rights, contact licensing@idwpublishing.com

19 18 17 16 1 2 3 4

Ted Adams, CEO & Publisher
Greg Goldstein, President & COO
Robbie Robbins, EVP/Sr. Graphic Artist
Matthew Ruzicka, CPA, Chief Financial Officer

IDW
www.IDWPUBLISHING.com

Dirk Wood, VP of Marketing
Lorelei Bunjes, VP of Digital Services
Jeff Webber, VP of Licensing, Digital and Subsidiary Rights
Jerry Bennington, VP of New Product Development

Originally published as LUNA THE VAMPIRE issues #1–3.

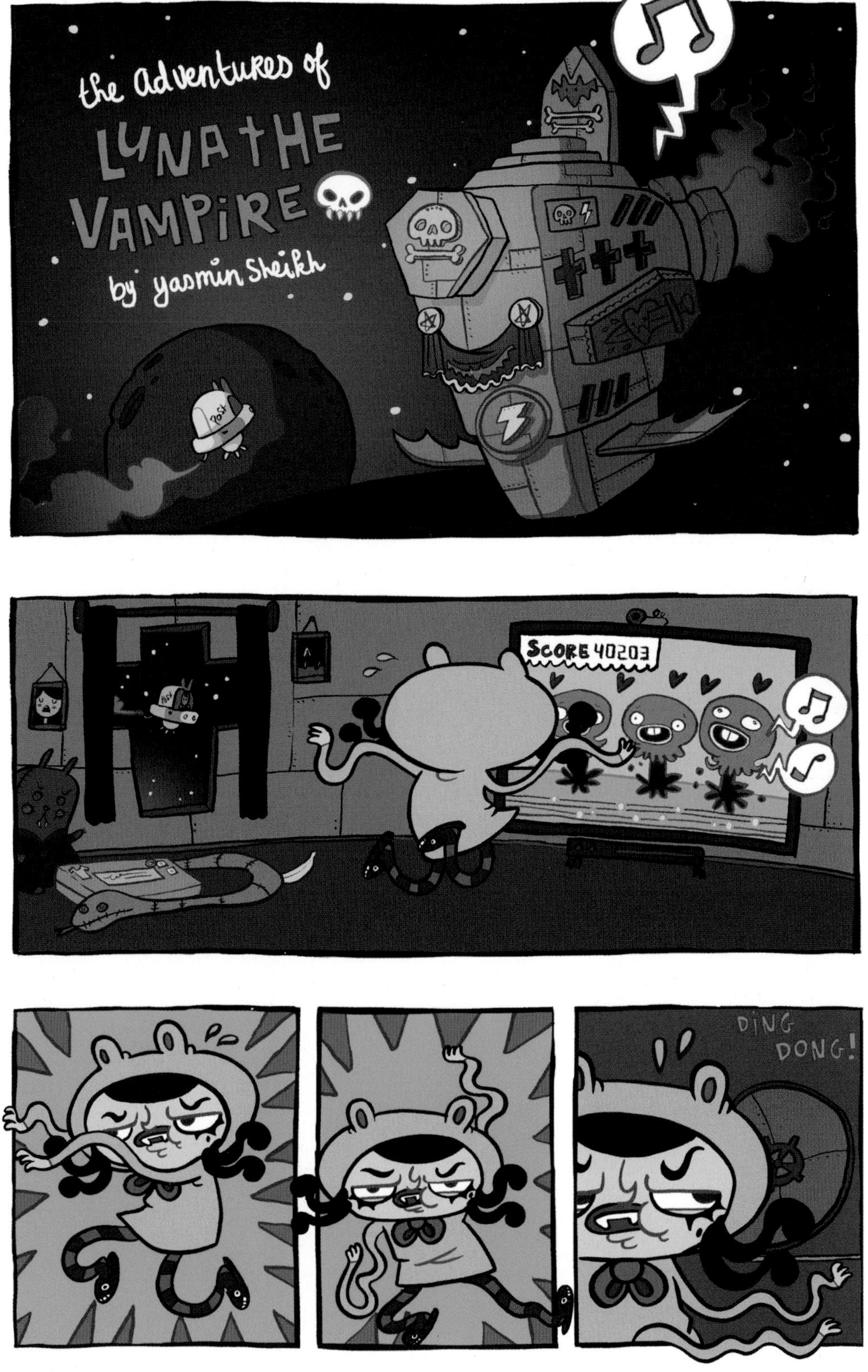
the adventures of
LUNA THE VAMPIRE
by yasmin Sheikh
POST
SCORE 40203
DING DONG!

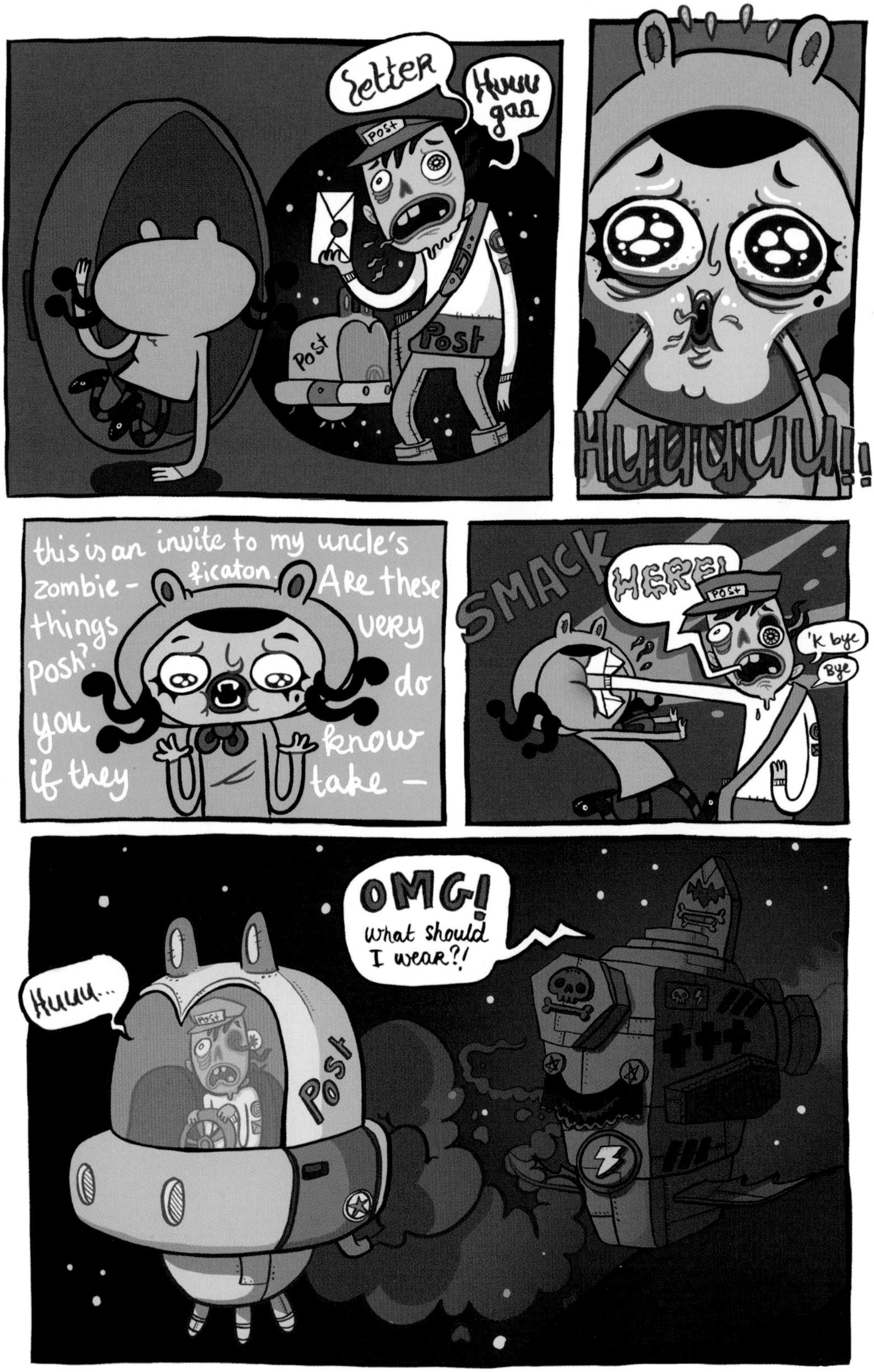

Letter
Huuu gaa
HUUUUUU!!
this is an invite to my uncle's zombie-ficaton. Are these things very posh? do you know if they take —
SMACK
HERE!
'K bye
Bye
OMG! What should I wear?!
Huuu...

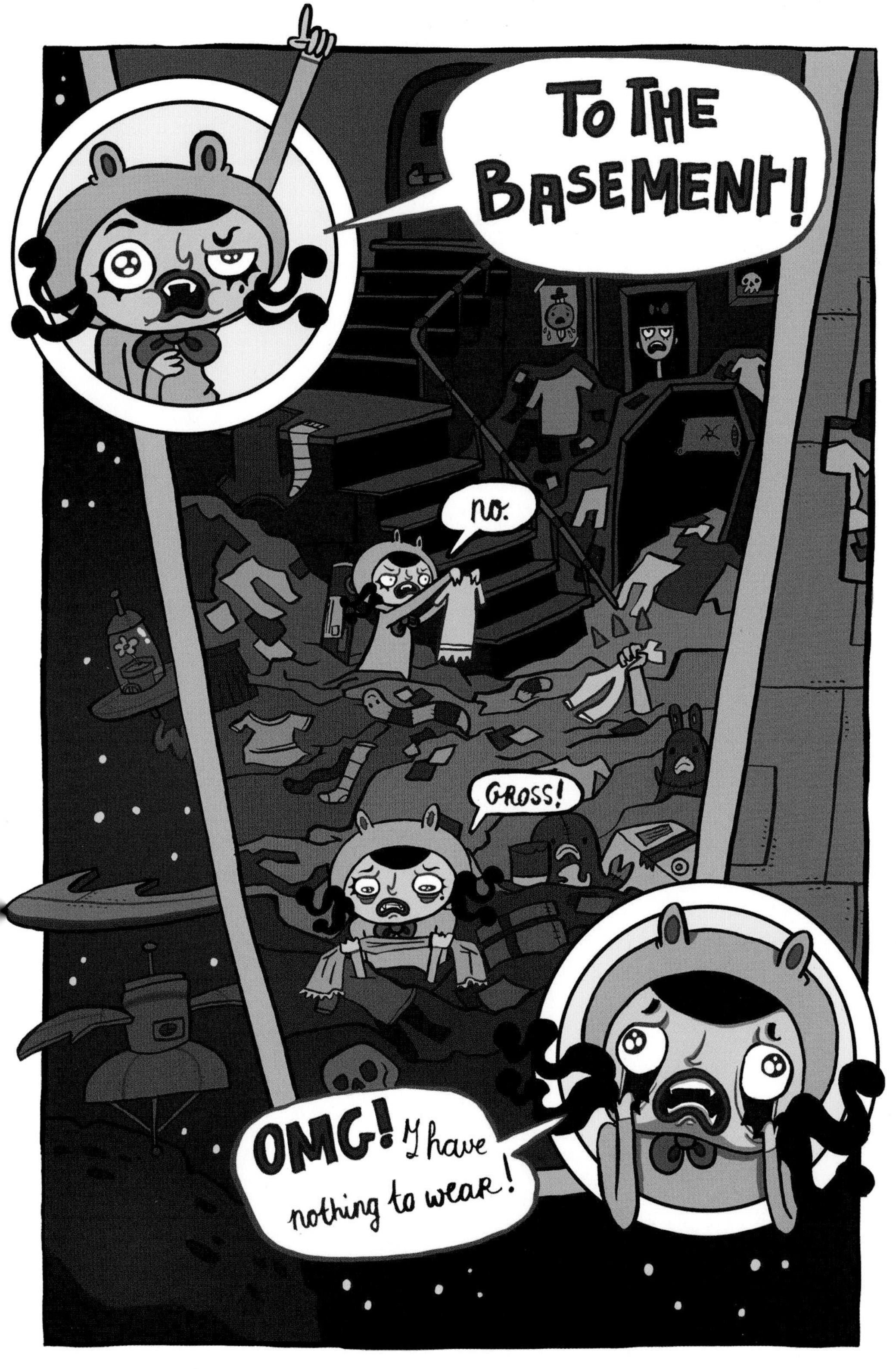
TO THE BASEMENT!
no.
GROSS!
OMG! I have nothing to wear!

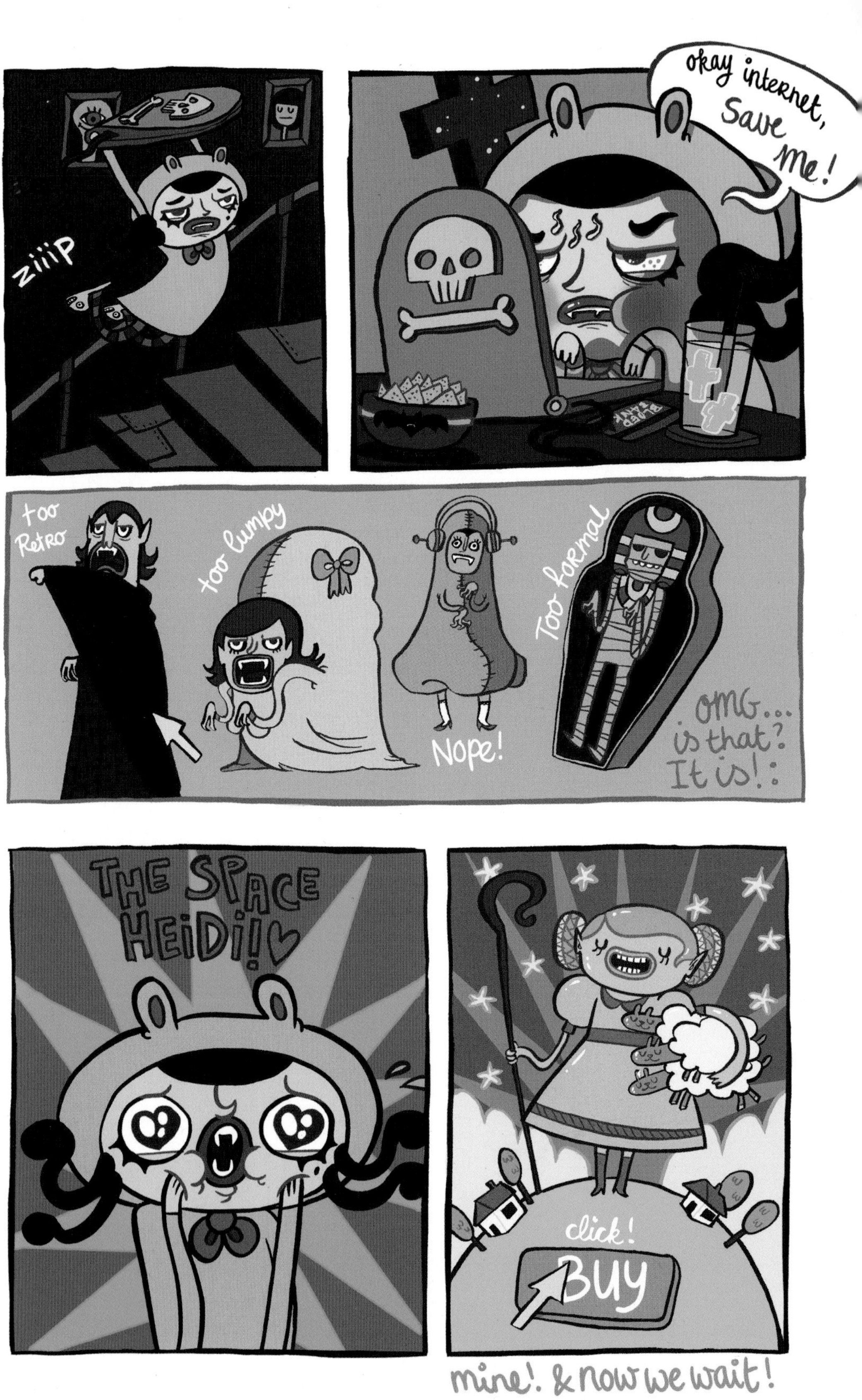
ziiip
okay internet, Save me!
too Retro
too lumpy
Nope!
Too formal
OMG... is that? It is!:
THE SPACE HEIDI!♡
click!
BUY
mine!. & now we wait!

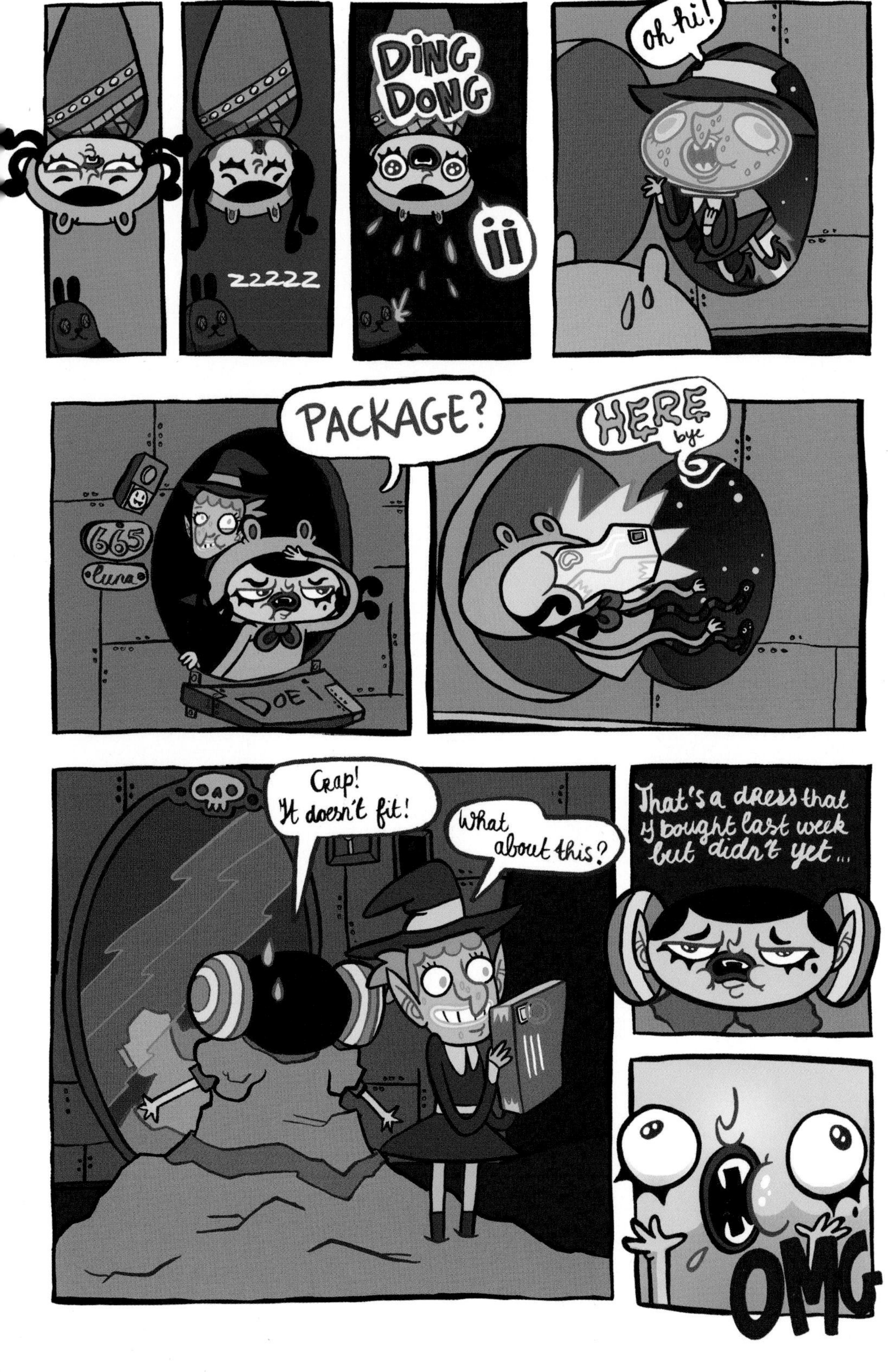
zzzzz
DING DONG
!!
oh hi!
PACKAGE?
665
luna
DOE!
HERE
bye
Crap! It doesn't fit!
What about this?
That's a dress that I bought last week but didn't yet...
OMG

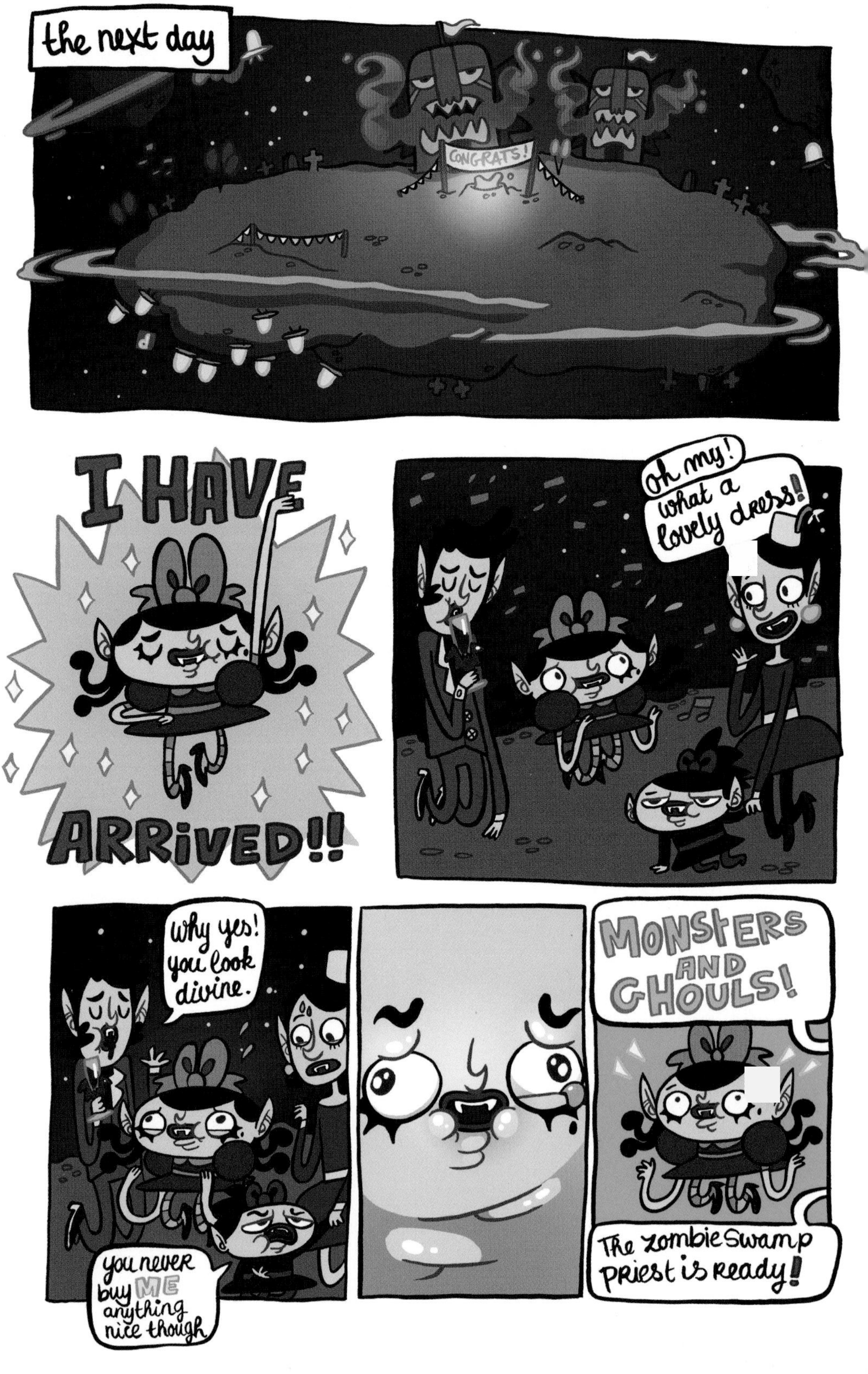
the next day
CONGRATS!
I HAVE ARRIVED!!
oh my! what a lovely dress!
Why yes! you look divine.
you never buy ME anything nice though
MONSTERS AND GHOULS!
The zombie Swamp priest is ready!

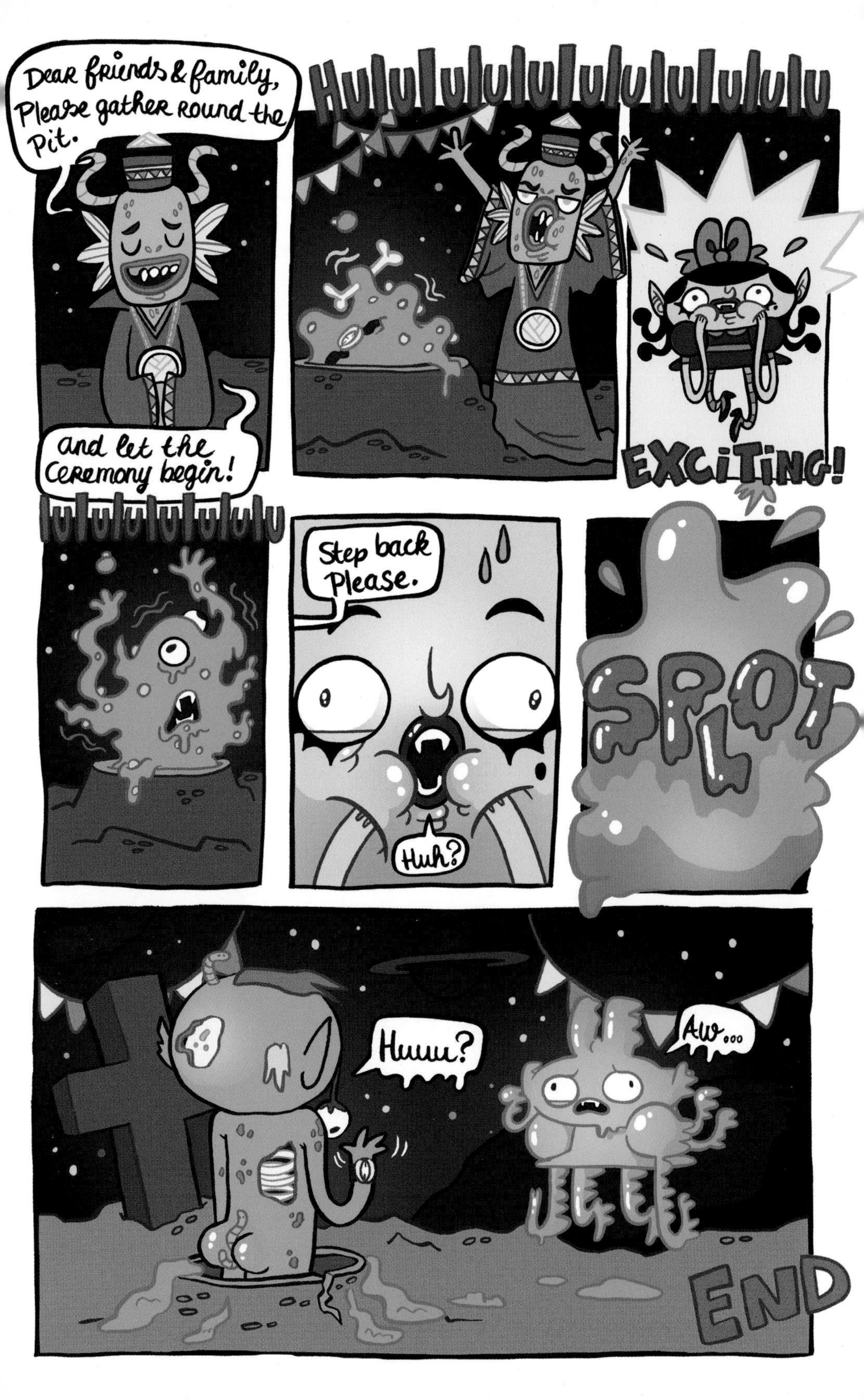
Dear friends & family, Please gather round the Pit.
and let the Ceremony begin!
Hululululululululululululu
lulululululululu
EXCiTiNG!
Step back Please.
Huh?
SPLOT
Huuu?
Aw...
END

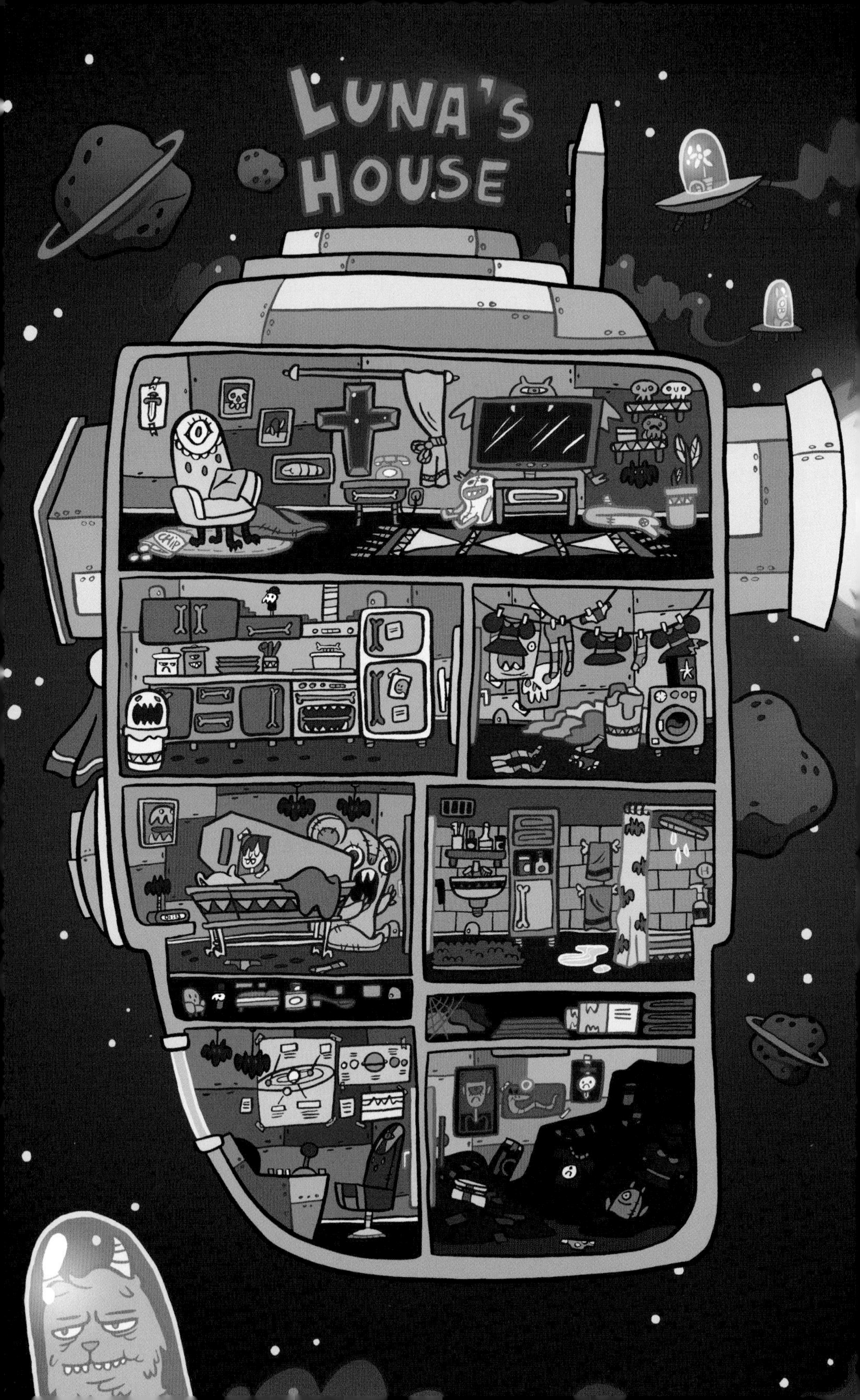
LUNA'S HOUSE
CHIP

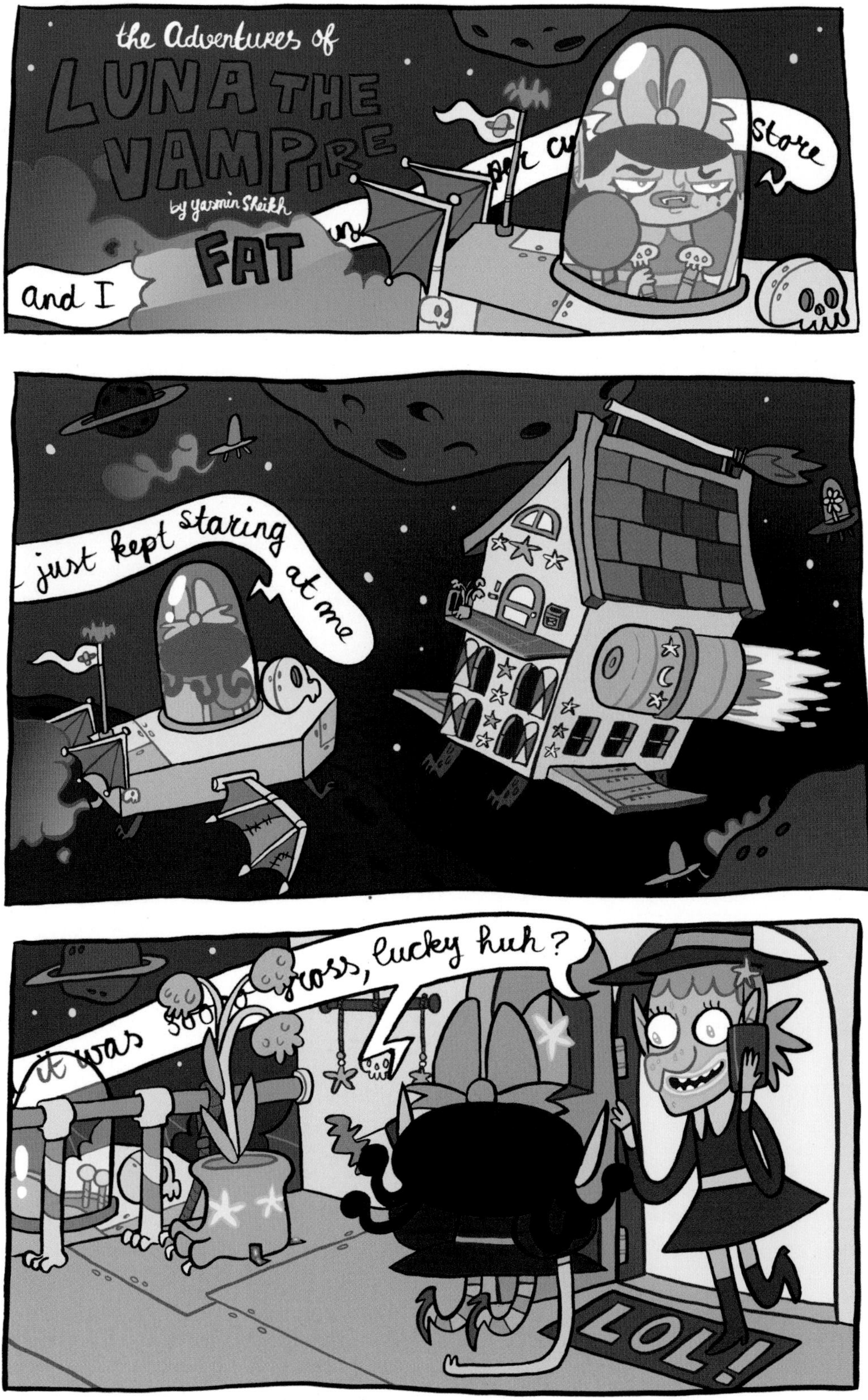

the Adventures of
LUNA THE VAMPIRE
by yasmin Sheikh
and I
FAT
per cu
store
just kept staring at me
it was
gross, lucky huh?
LOL!

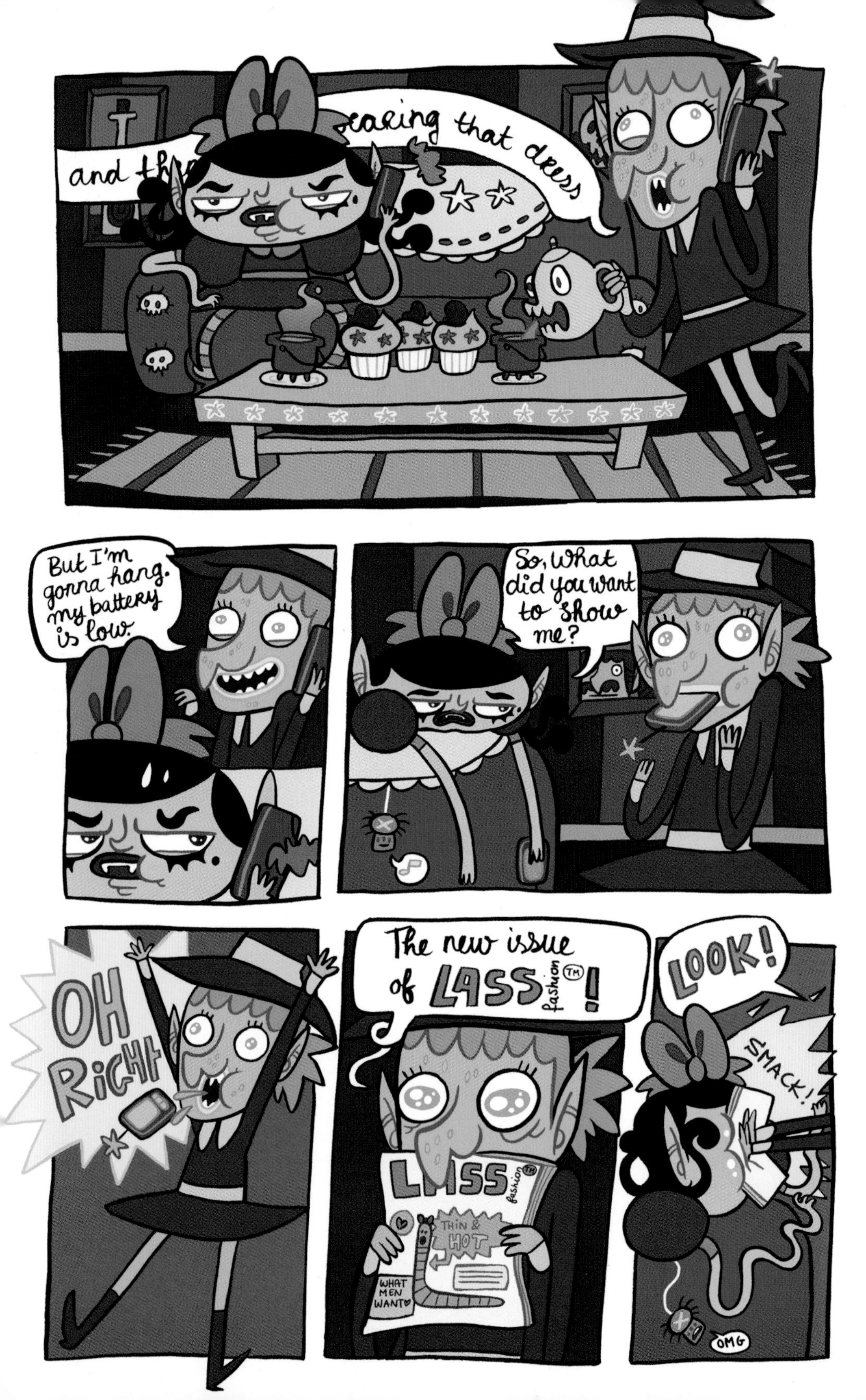
and th
earing that dress
But I'm gonna hang. my battery is low.
So, What did you want to show me?
OH RIGHT
The new issue of LASS fashion™!
LASS fashion™
THIN & HOT
WHAT MEN WANT♥
LOOK!
SMACK!
OMG

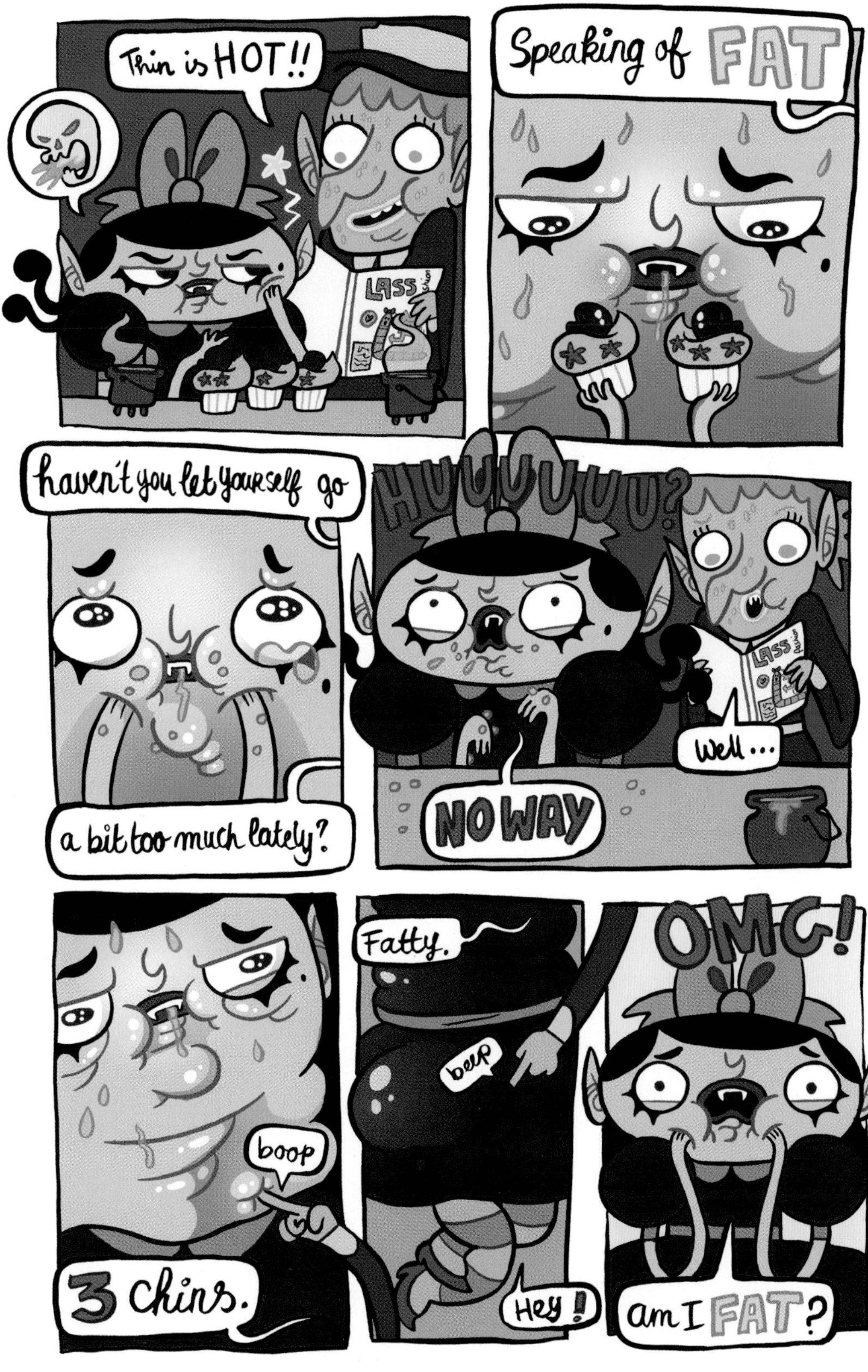
Thin is HOT!!
LASS
Speaking of FAT
haven't you let yourself go
a bit too much lately?
HUUUUUUU?
Well...
NO WAY
boop
3 chins.
Fatty.
beep
Hey!
OMG!
am I FAT?

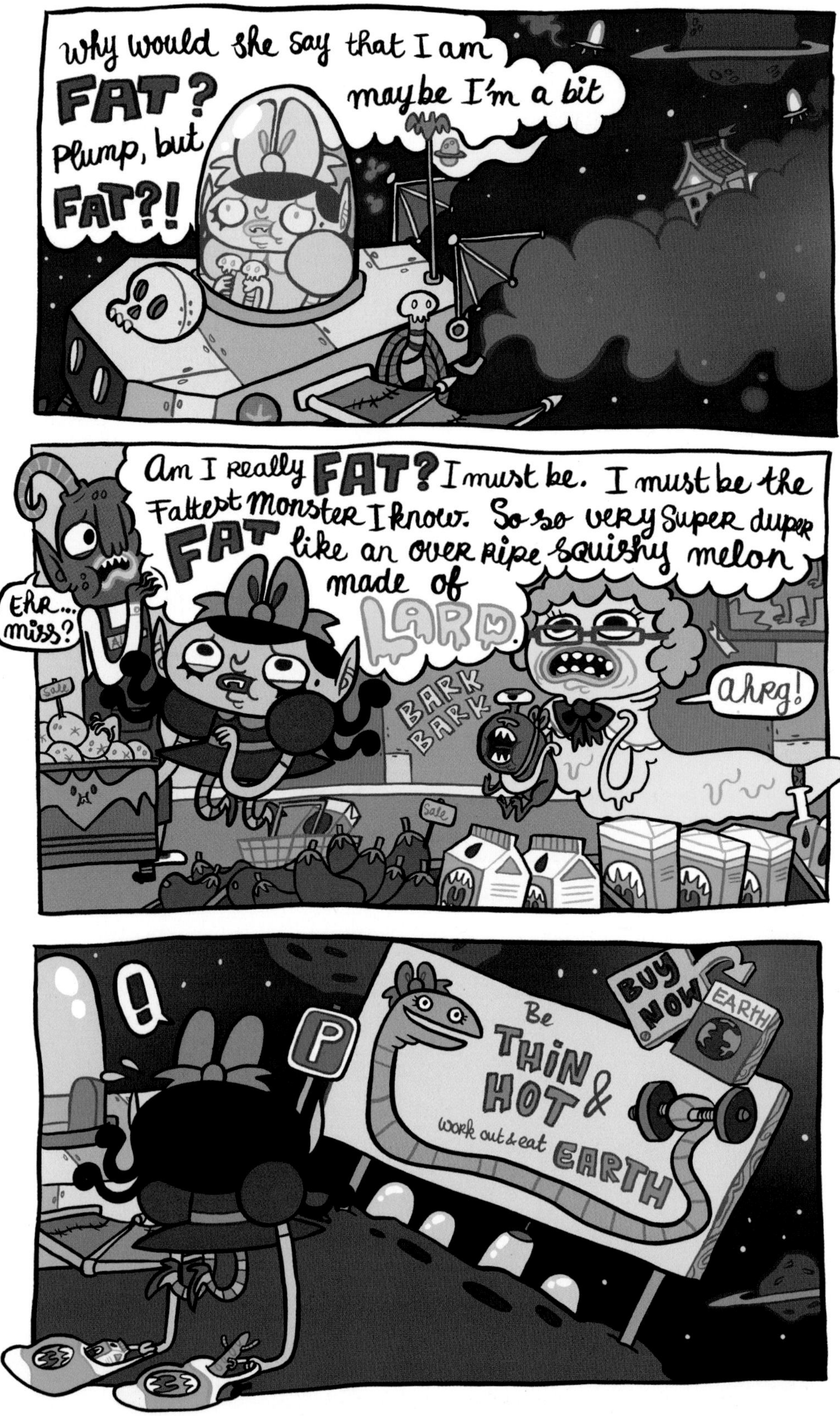
Why would she say that I am
FAT?
maybe I'm a bit
Plump, but
FAT?!
Am I really FAT? I must be. I must be the Fattest Monster I know. So so very super duper FAT like an over ripe squishy melon made of LARD.
Ehr... miss?
Sale
BARK BARK
ahrg!
Sale
!
P
Be THIN & HOT
work out & eat EARTH
BUY NOW
EARTH

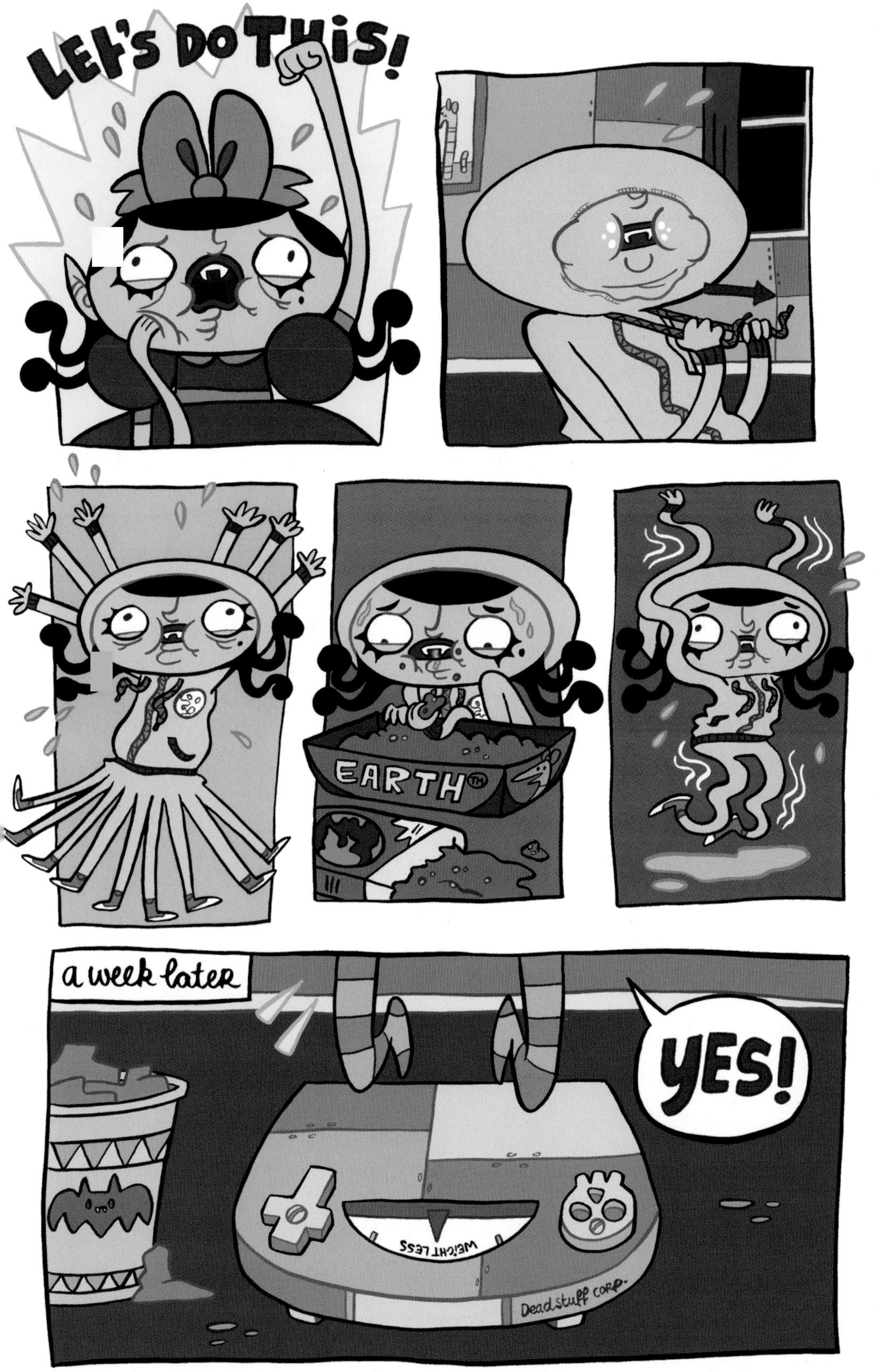
LET'S DO THIS!
EARTH™
a week later
YES!
WEIGHT LESS
Deadstuff CORP.

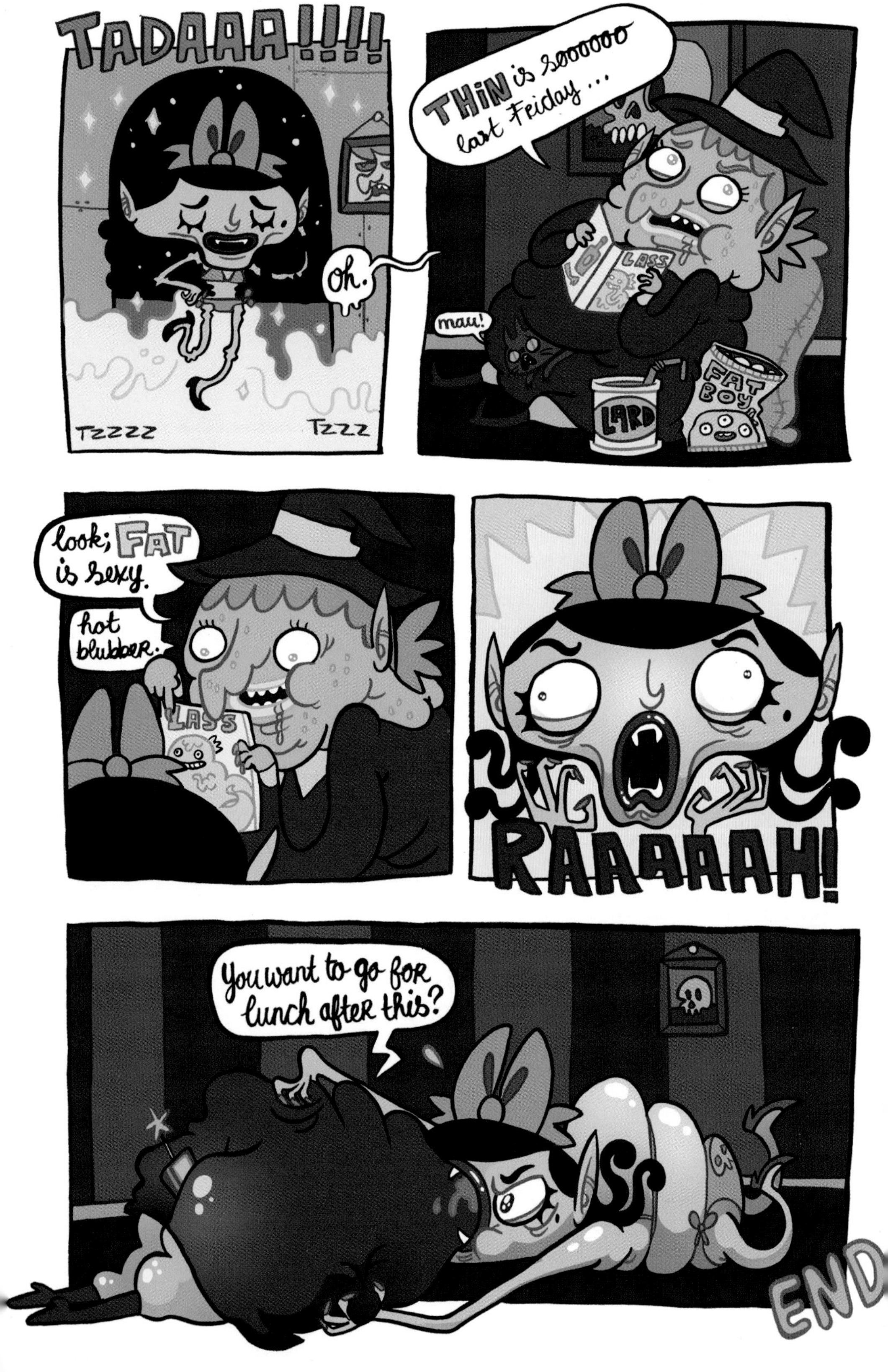
TADAAA!!!!
Oh.
TZZZZ
TZZZ
THIN is sooooo last Friday ...
LASS
mau!
LARD
FAT BOY
look; FAT is sexy.
hot blubber.
LASS
RAAAAAH!
You want to go for lunch after this?
END

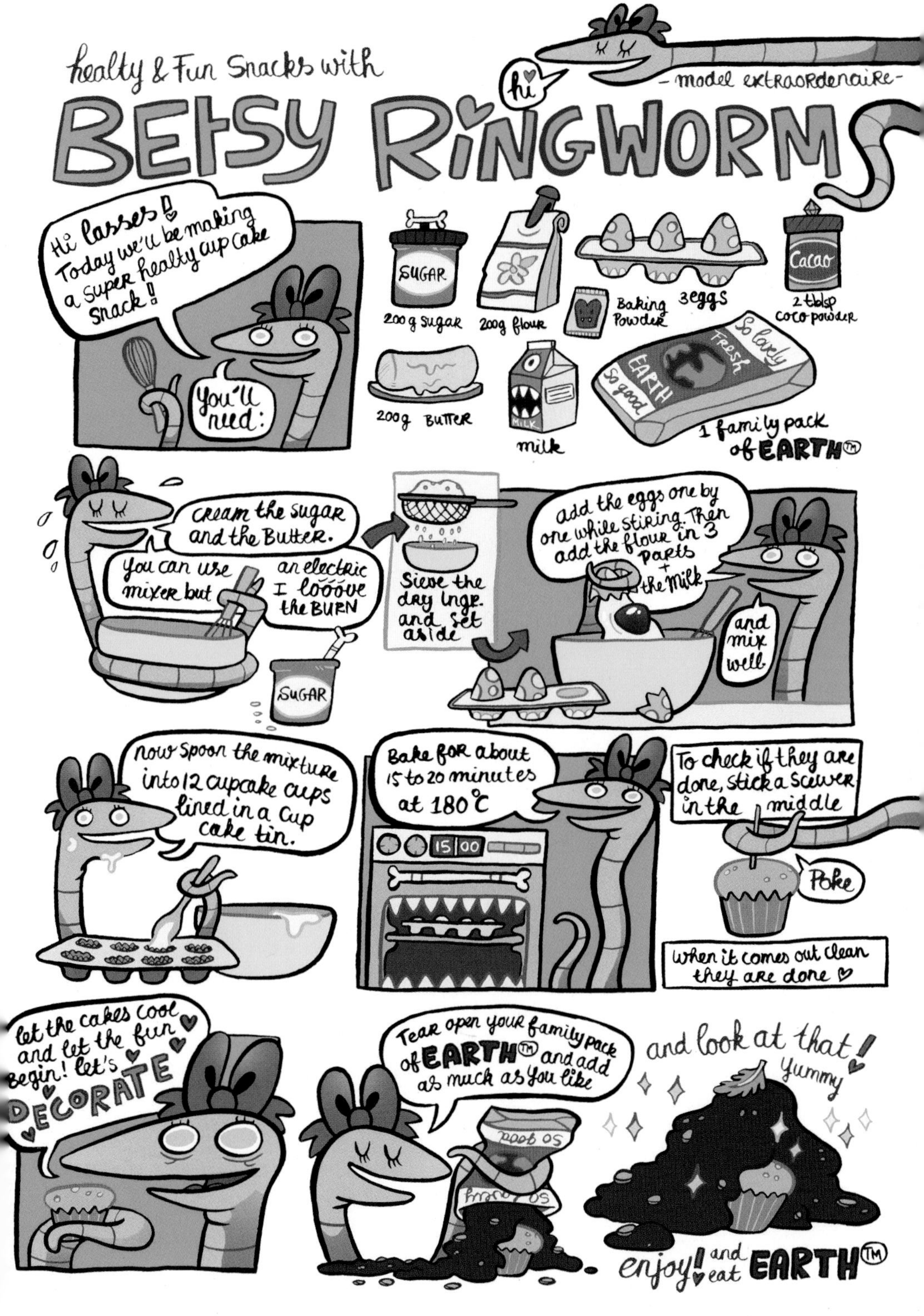
healty & Fun Snacks with
BETSY RINGWORM
hi
-model extraordenaire-
Hi lasses! Today we'll be making a super healty cup cake snack!
You'll need:
SUGAR
200g sugar
200g flour
Baking Powder
3 eggs
Cacao
2 tblsp coco powder
200g BUTTER
MILK
milk
EARTH Fresh So lovely So good
1 family pack of EARTH™
Cream the sugar and the Butter.
You can use an electric mixer but I looove the BURN
SUGAR
Sieve the dry ingr. and set aside
add the eggs one by one while stiring. Then add the flour in 3 parts + the milk
and mix well
now spoon the mixture into 12 cupcake cups lined in a Cup cake tin.
Bake for about 15 to 20 minutes at 180°C
15|00
To check if they are done, stick a scewer in the middle
Poke
when it comes out clean they are done
let the cakes cool and let the fun begin! let's DECORATE
Tear open your family pack of EARTH™ and add as much as you like
and look at that!
Yummy
enjoy! and eat EARTH™

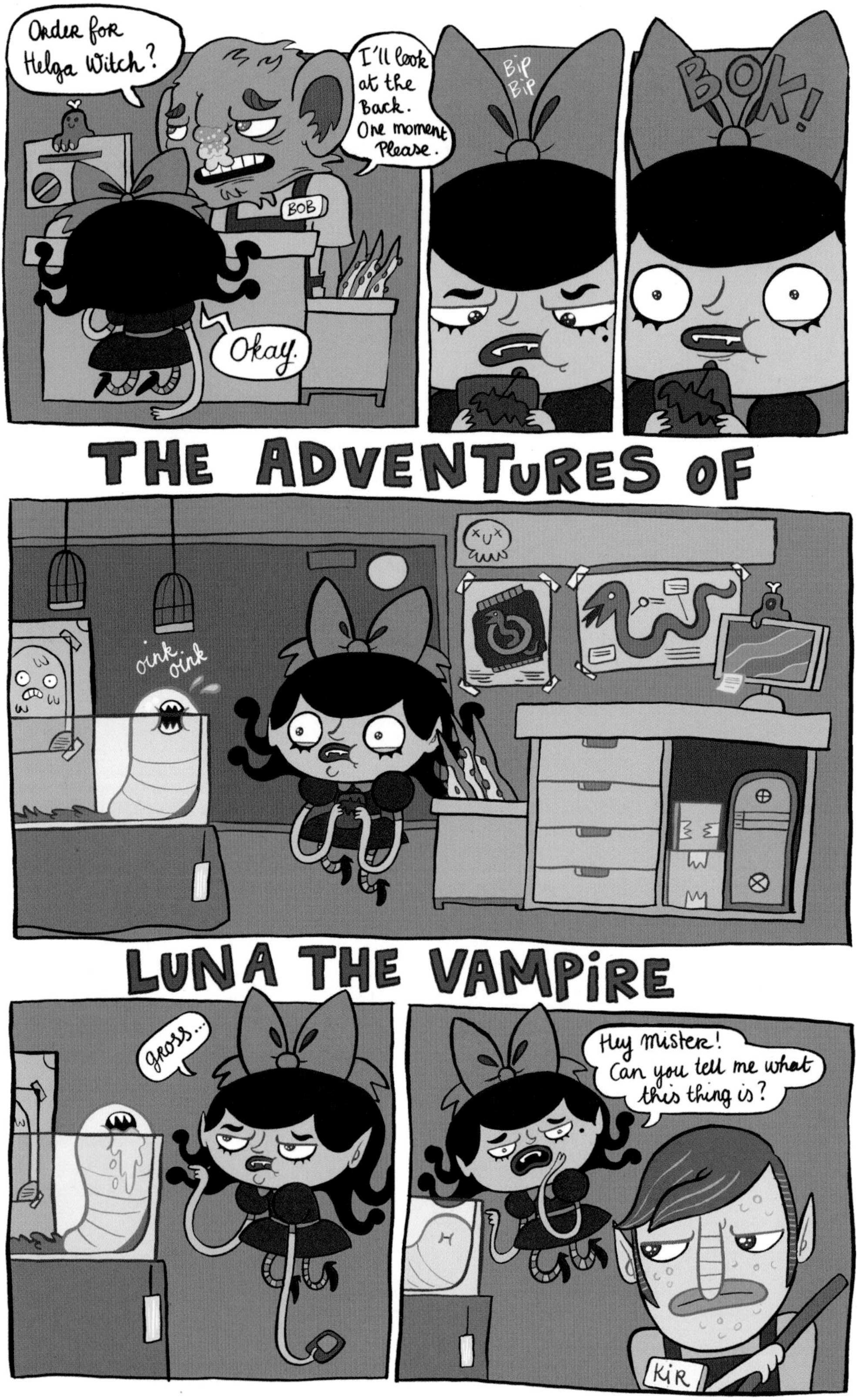
Order for Helga Witch?
BOB
I'll look at the Back. One moment Please.
Okay.
Bip Bip
BOK!
THE ADVENTURES OF
oink oink
LUNA THE VAMPIRE
GROSS...
Hey mister! Can you tell me what this thing is?
KIR

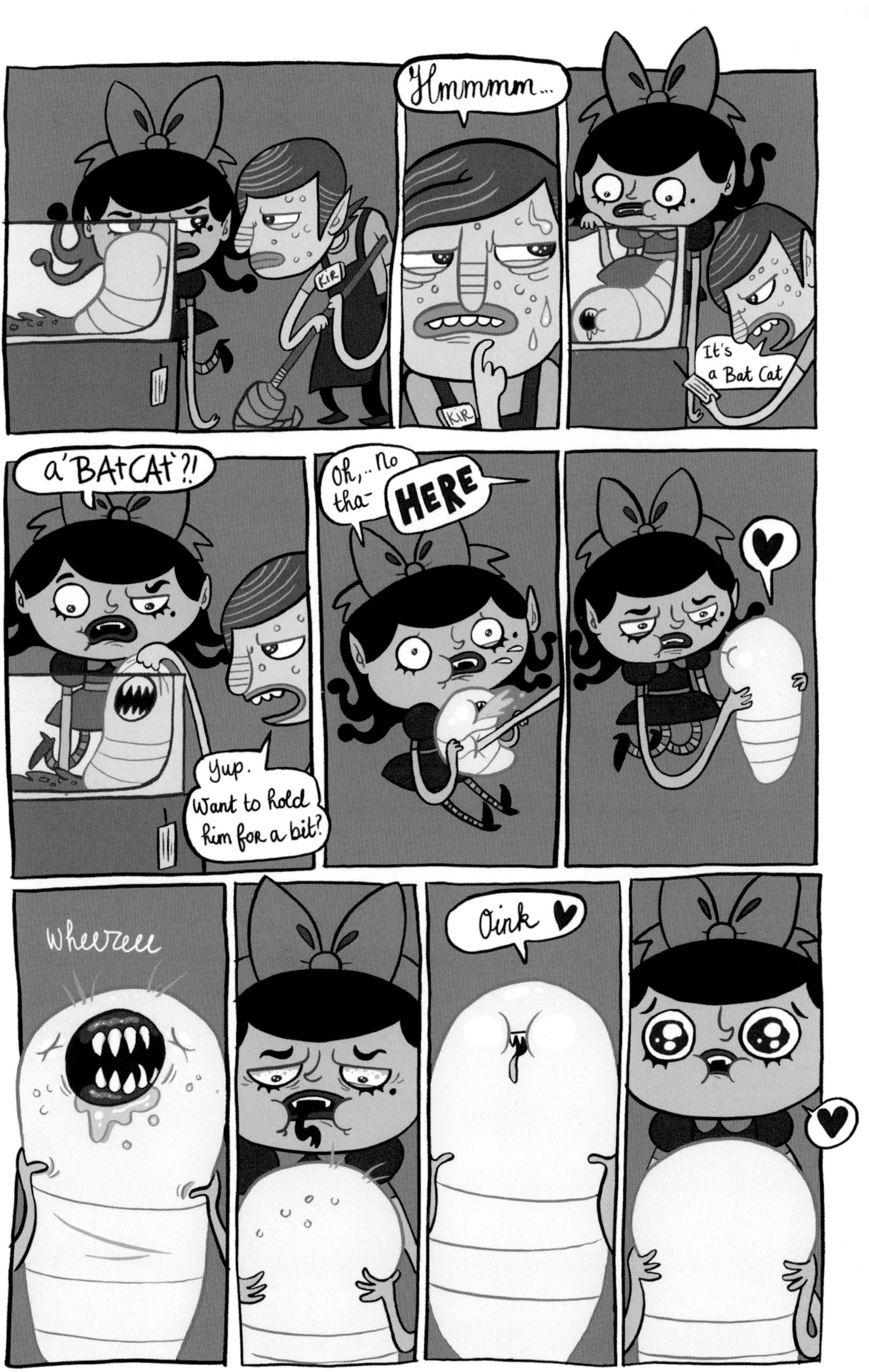

Hmmmm...
It's a Bat Cat
a'BAtCAt'?!
Yup. Want to hold him for a bit?
Oh,.. no tha-
HERE
wheezeee
Oink

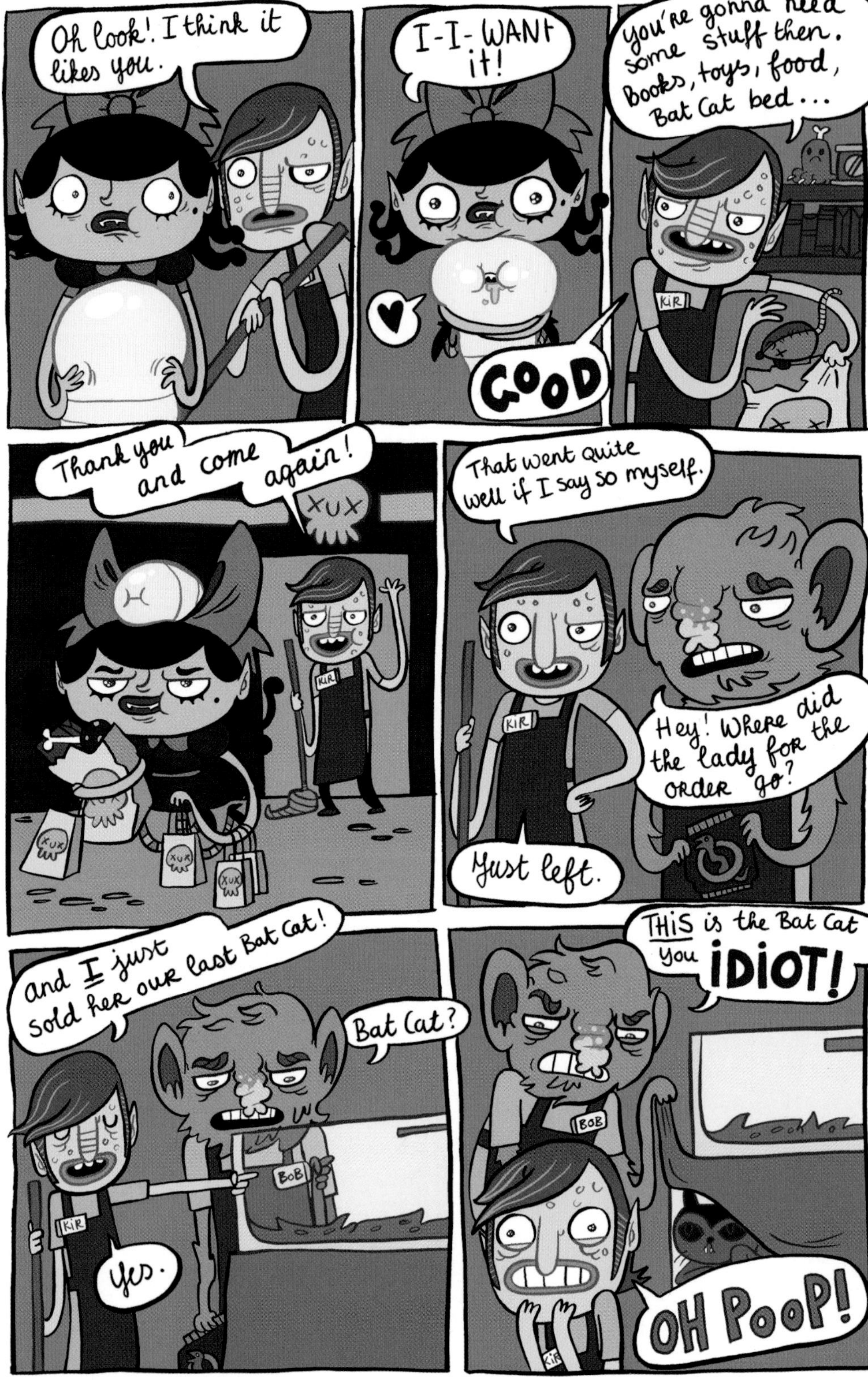
Oh look! I think it likes you.
I-I- WANT it!
GOOD
You're gonna need some stuff then. Books, toys, food, Bat Cat bed...
KIR
Thank you and come again!
XUX
KIR
That went quite well if I say so myself.
KIR
Hey! Where did the lady for the order go?
Just left.
And I just sold her our last Bat Cat!
Bat Cat?
BOB
KIR
Yes.
THIS is the Bat Cat you IDIOT!
BOB
OH POOP!

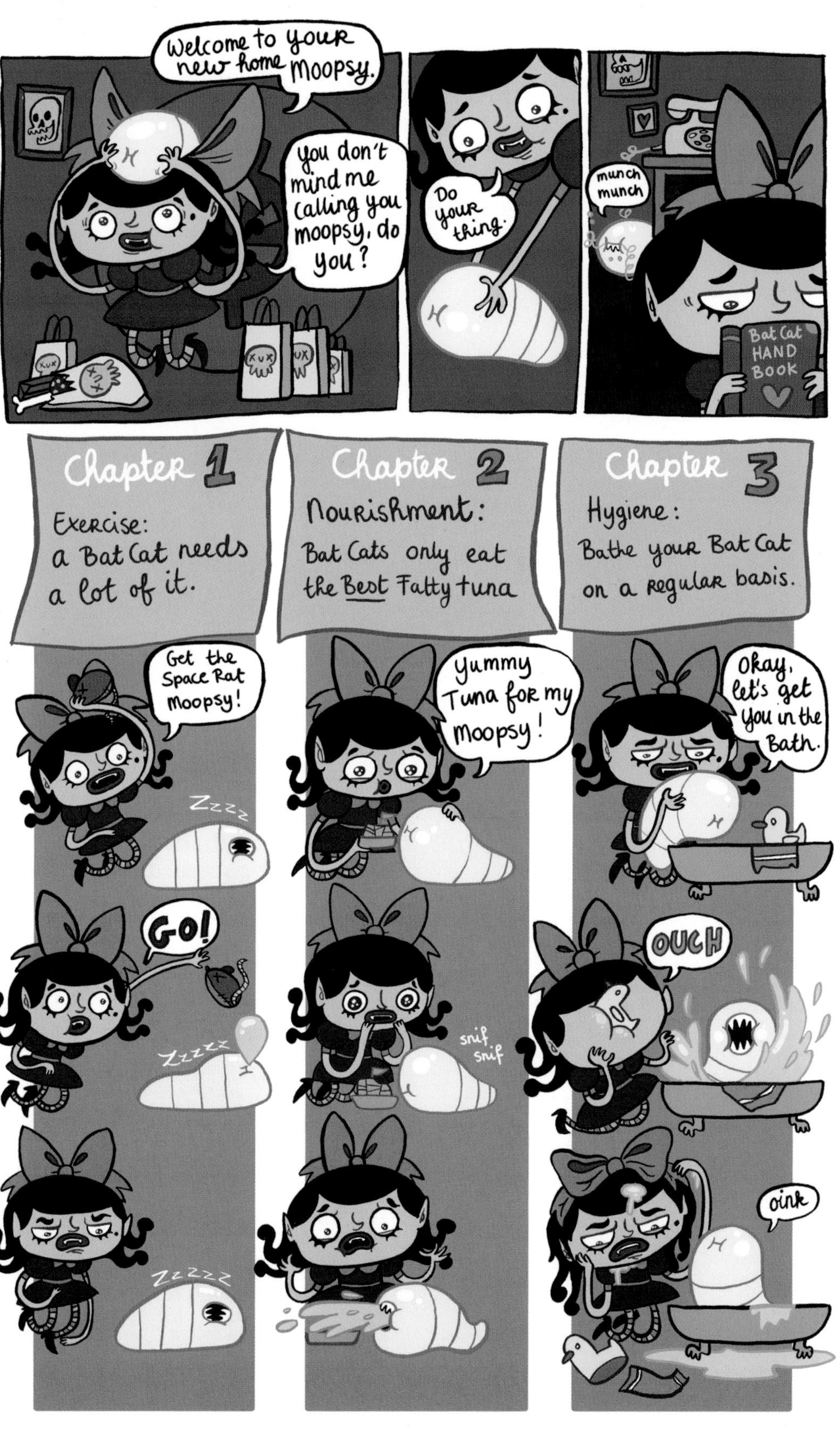
Welcome to your new home moopsy.
You don't mind me calling you moopsy, do you?
Do your thing.
munch munch
Bat Cat HAND BOOK
Chapter 1
Exercise: a Bat Cat needs a lot of it.
Chapter 2
Nourishment: Bat Cats only eat the Best Fatty tuna
Chapter 3
Hygiene: Bathe your Bat Cat on a regular basis.
Get the Space Rat Moopsy!
Zzzz
GO!
Zzzzz
Zzzzz
Yummy Tuna for my Moopsy!
snif snif
Okay, let's get you in the Bath.
OUCH
oink

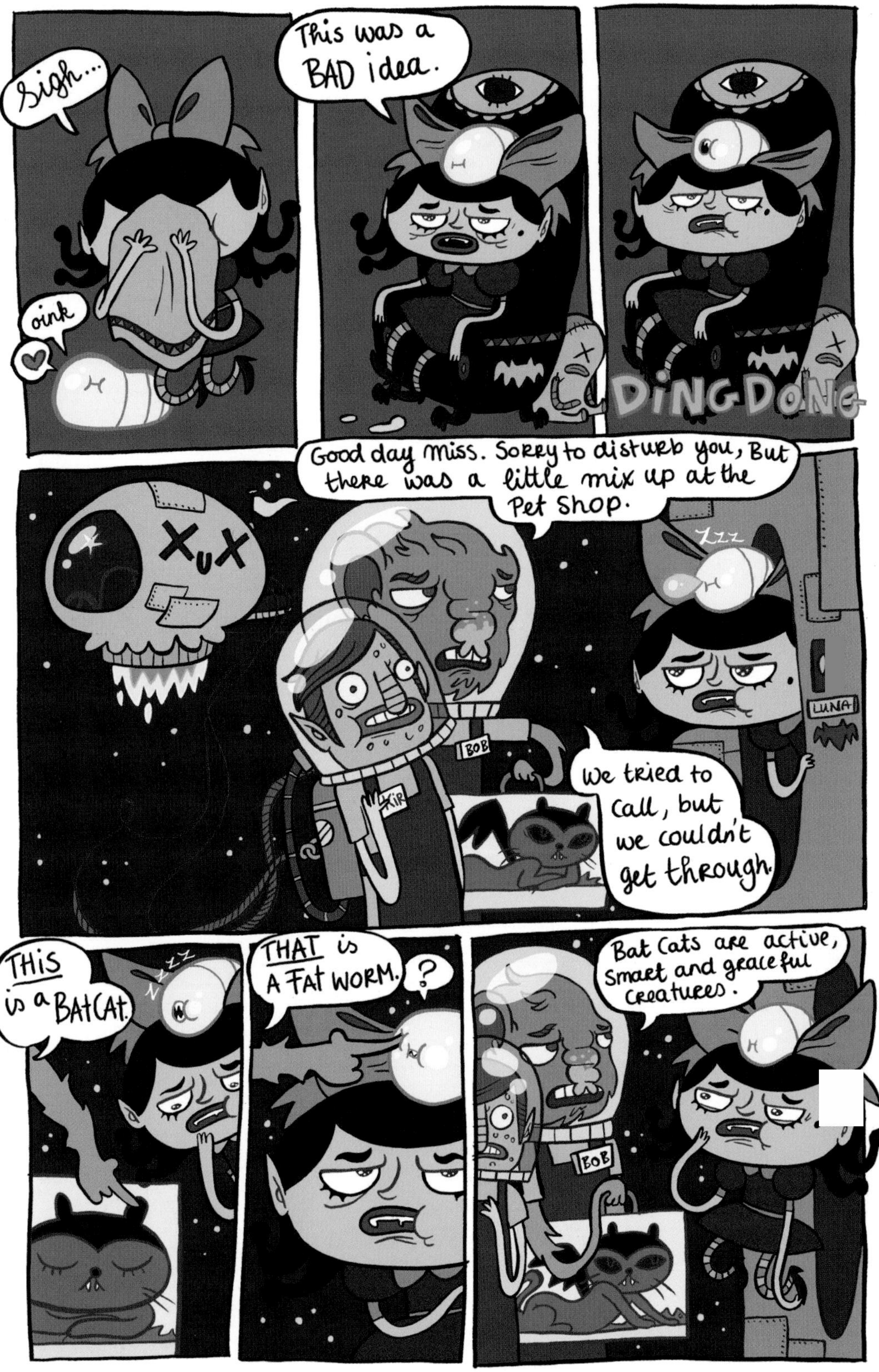
Sigh...
oink
This was a BAD idea.
DINGDONG
Good day miss. Sorry to disturb you, But there was a little mix up at the Pet Shop.
ZZZ
LUNA
BOB
XIR
We tried to call, but we couldn't get through.
THIS is a BATCAT.
THAT is A FAT WORM.
?
Bat Cats are active, smart and graceful creatures.
BOB

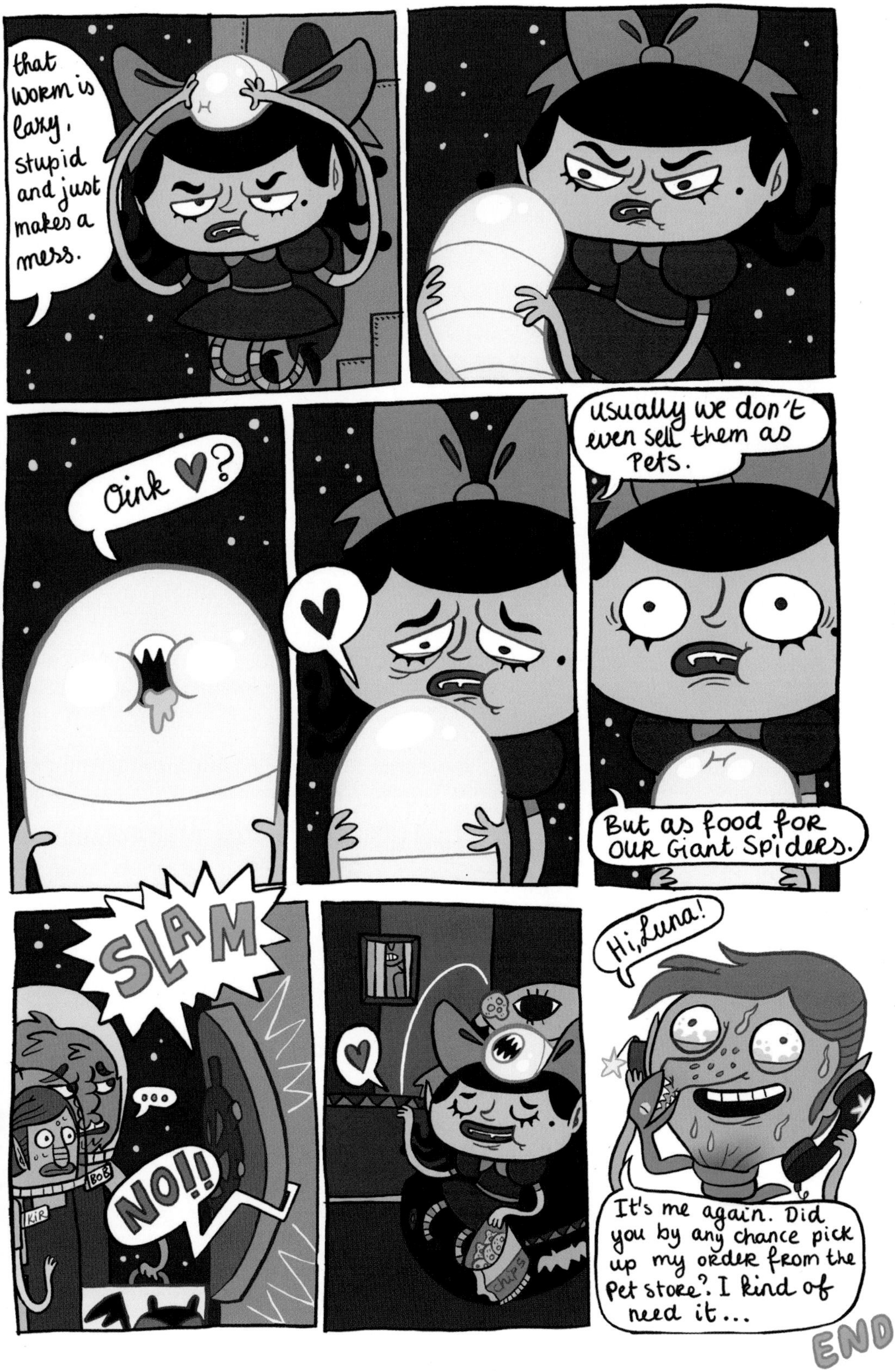
that worm is lazy, stupid and just makes a mess.
Oink ♥?
usually we don't even sell them as pets.
But as food for our Giant Spiders.
SLAM
...
BOB
KIR
NO!!
CHIPS
Hi, Luna!
It's me again. Did you by any chance pick up my order from the pet store? I kind of need it...
END

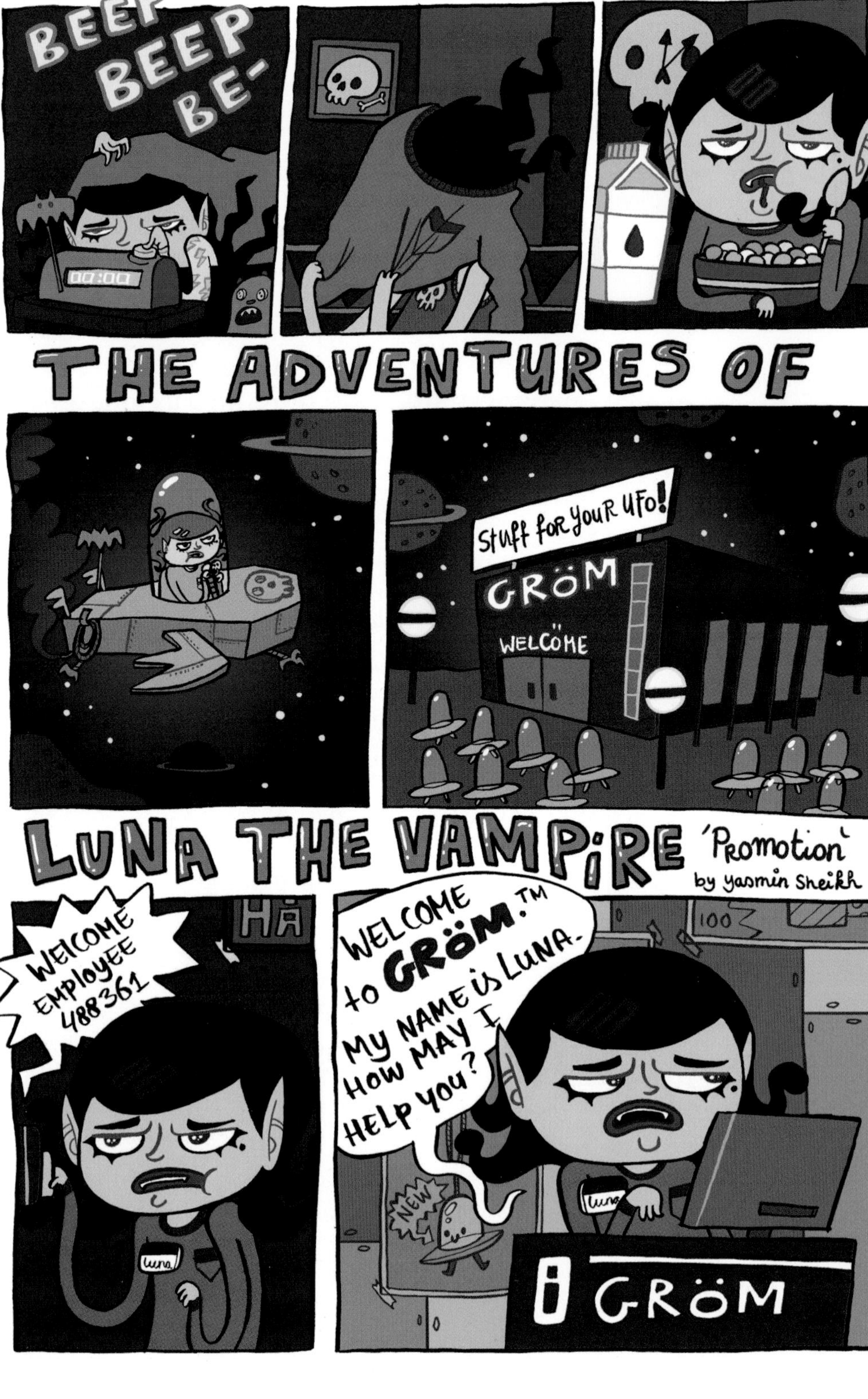
BEEP BEEP BE-
00:00
THE ADVENTURES OF
Stuff for your UFO!
GRÖM
WELCOME
LUNA THE VAMPIRE
'Promotion'
by yasmin sheikh
WELCOME EMPLOYEE 488361
luna
WELCOME to GRÖM.™ My NAME is LUNA. How MAY I HELP you?
100
NEW
luna
GRÖM

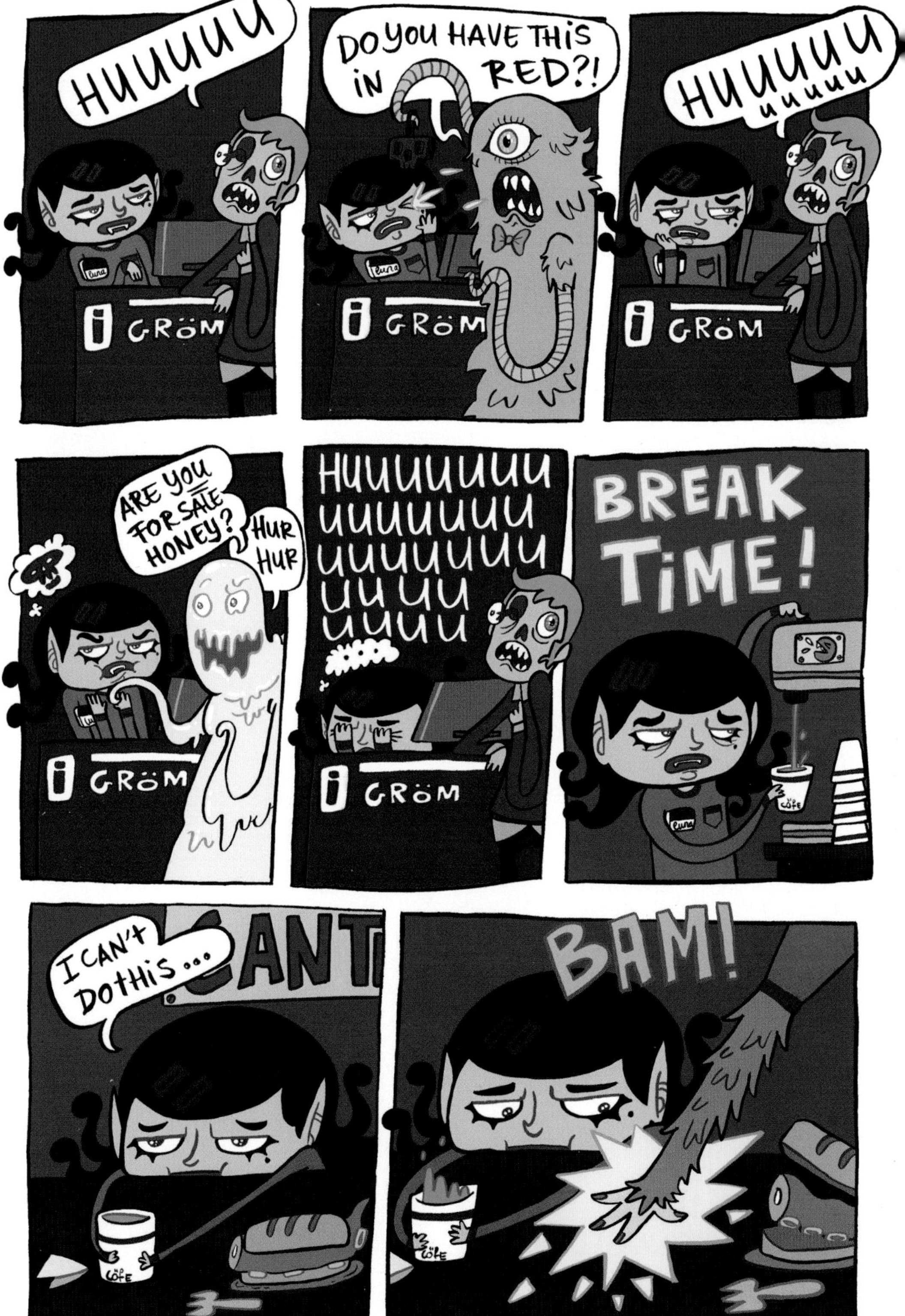
HUUUUU
luna
GRÖM
DO YOU HAVE THIS IN RED?!
luna
GRÖM
HUUUUU uuuuu
GRÖM
ARE YOU FOR SALE HONEY?
HUR HUR
GRÖM
HUUUUUUUU
UUUUUUUU
UUUUUUUU
UU UU
UUUU
GRÖM
BREAK TIME!
luna
CAFE
I CAN'T DO THIS...
ANT
CAFE
BAM!
CAFE

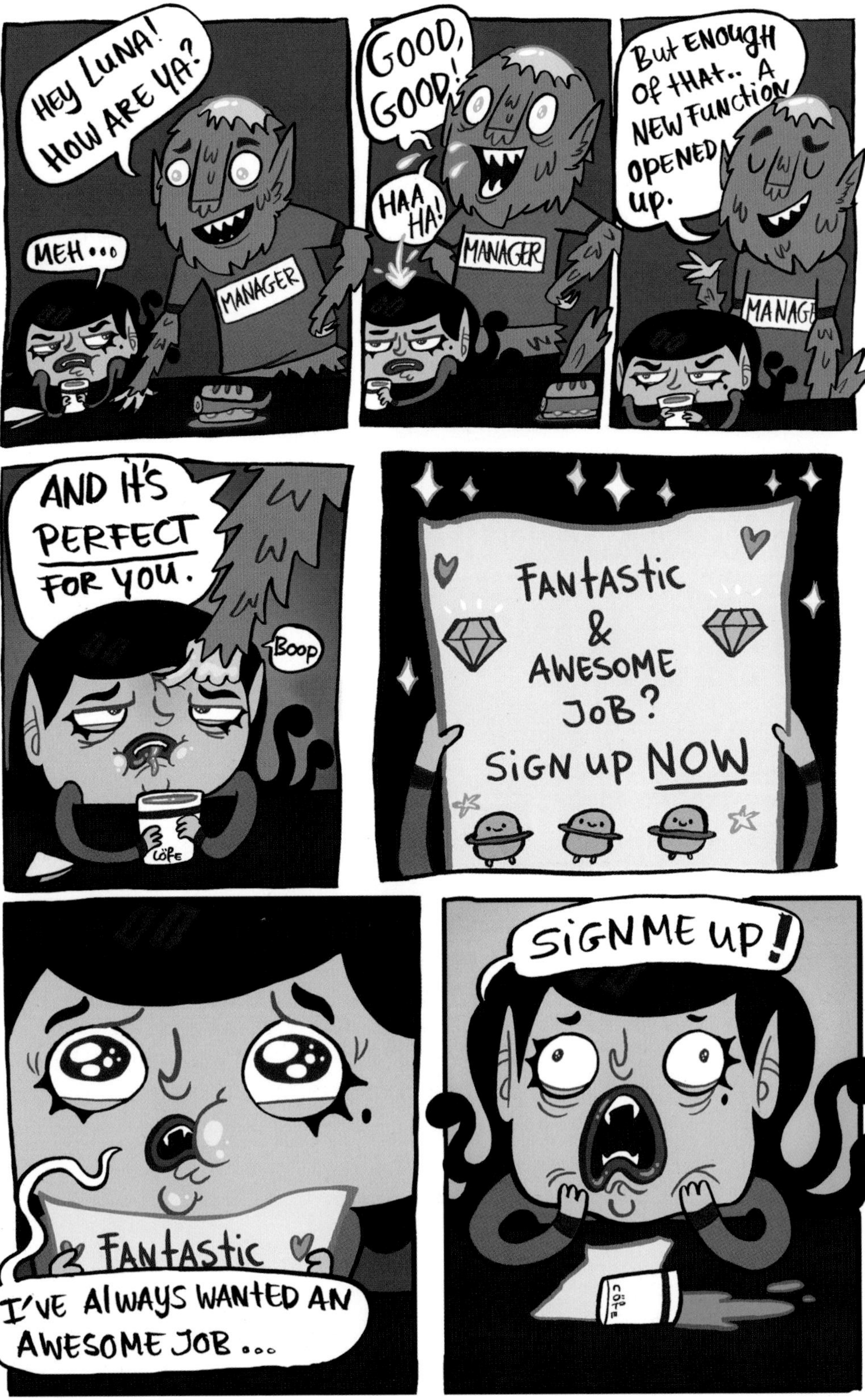
HEY LUNA! HOW ARE YA?
MEH...
GOOD, GOOD!
HAA HA!
MANAGER
But ENOUGH OF THAT.. A NEW FUNCTION OPENED UP.
AND IT'S PERFECT FOR YOU.
BOOP
FANTASTIC & AWESOME JOB? SIGN UP NOW
SIGN ME UP!
FANTASTIC
I'VE ALWAYS WANTED AN AWESOME JOB...

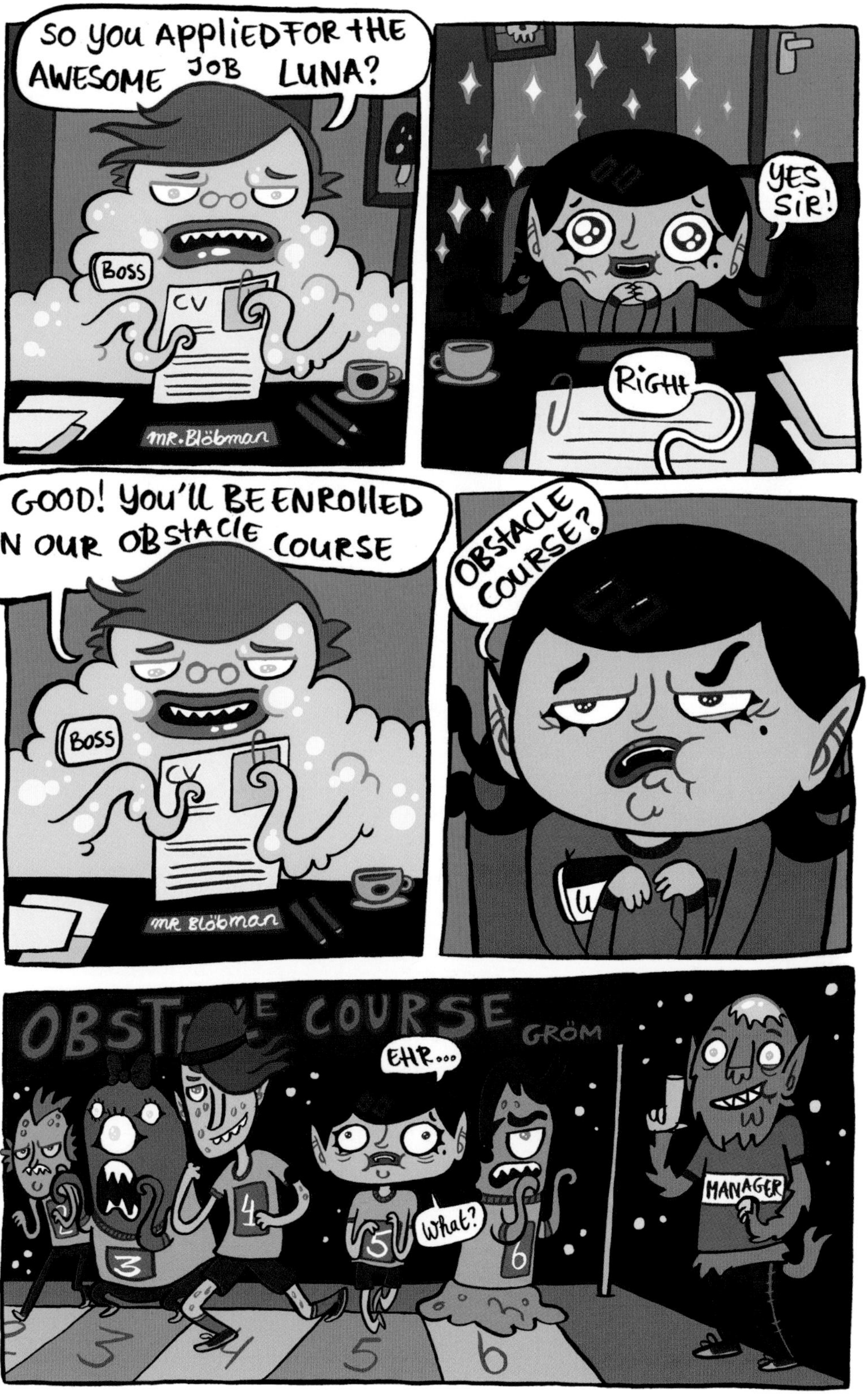
SO YOU APPLIED FOR THE AWESOME JOB LUNA?
BOSS
CV
MR. Blöbman
YES SIR!
RIGHT
GOOD! YOU'LL BE ENROLLED IN OUR OBSTACLE COURSE
BOSS
CV
MR Blöbman
OBSTACLE COURSE?
GRÖM
EHR...
What?
MANAGER

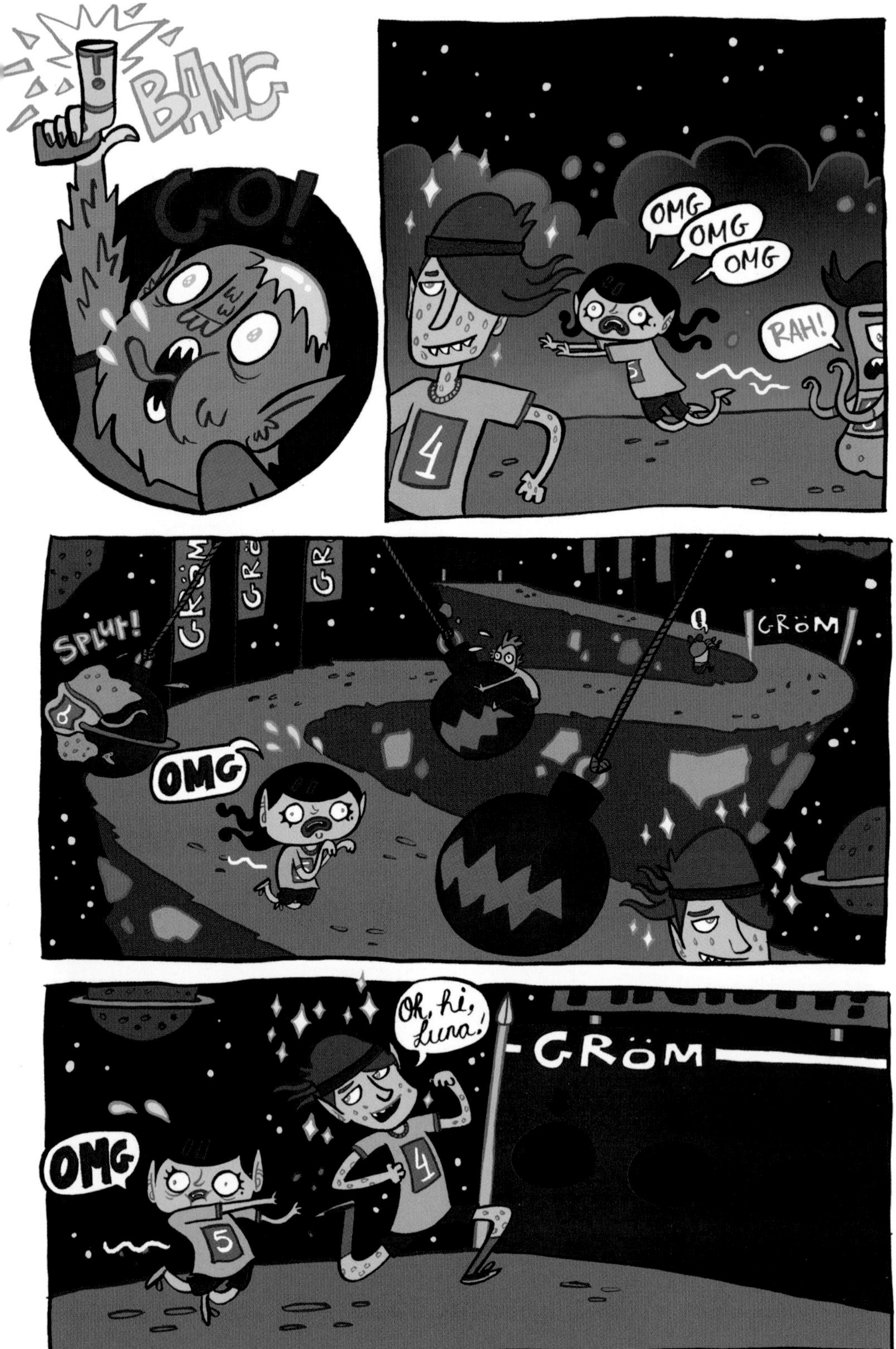
BANG
GO!
OMG
OMG
OMG
RAH!
SPLUT!
GRÖM
GRÖ
GR
GRÖM
OMG
OMG
Oh, hi, Luna!
GRÖM

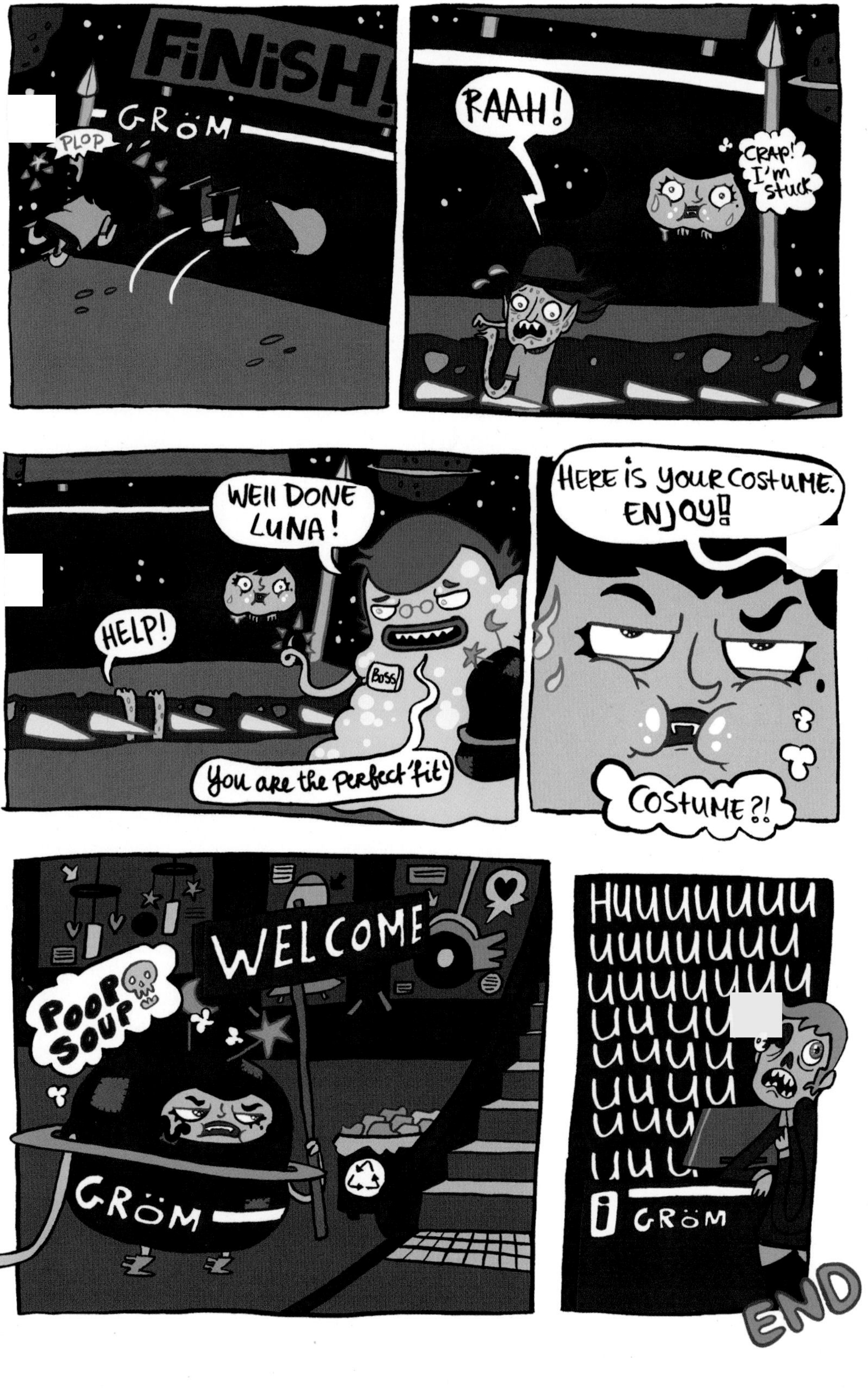

FINISH!
GRÖM
PLOP
RAAH!
CRAP! I'm stuck
Well DONE LUNA!
HELP!
BOSS
You are the perfect 'fit'
HERE IS YOUR COSTUME. ENJOY!!
COSTUME?!
WELCOME
POOP SOUP
GRÖM
HUUUUUUU
UUUUUUUU
UUUUUUUU
UUUUU
UUUUU
UUUUU
UUUU
UUU
GRÖM
END

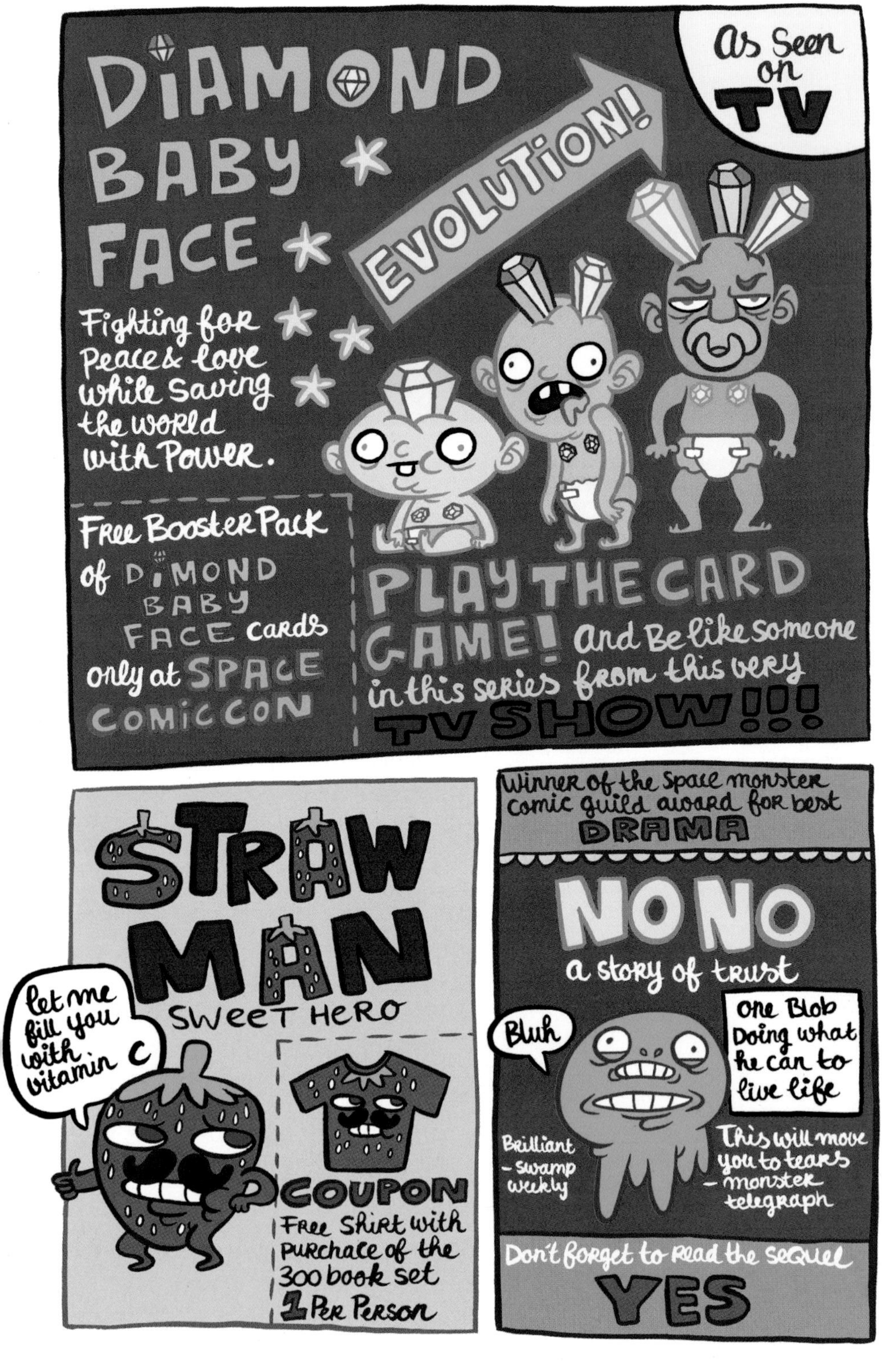
DIAMOND BABY FACE
EVOLUTION!
As Seen on TV
Fighting for Peace & love while saving the world with Power.
Free Booster Pack of DIMOND BABY FACE cards only at SPACE COMIC CON
PLAY THE CARD GAME! and Be like someone in this series from this very TV SHOW!!!
STRAW MAN
SWEET HERO
let me fill you with vitamin C
COUPON
Free Shirt with purchace of the 300 book set
1 Per Person
Winner of the Space monster comic guild award for best DRAMA
NO NO
a story of trust
Bluh
One Blob Doing what he can to live life
Brilliant - swamp weekly
This will move you to tears - monster telegraph
Don't forget to read the sequel
YES

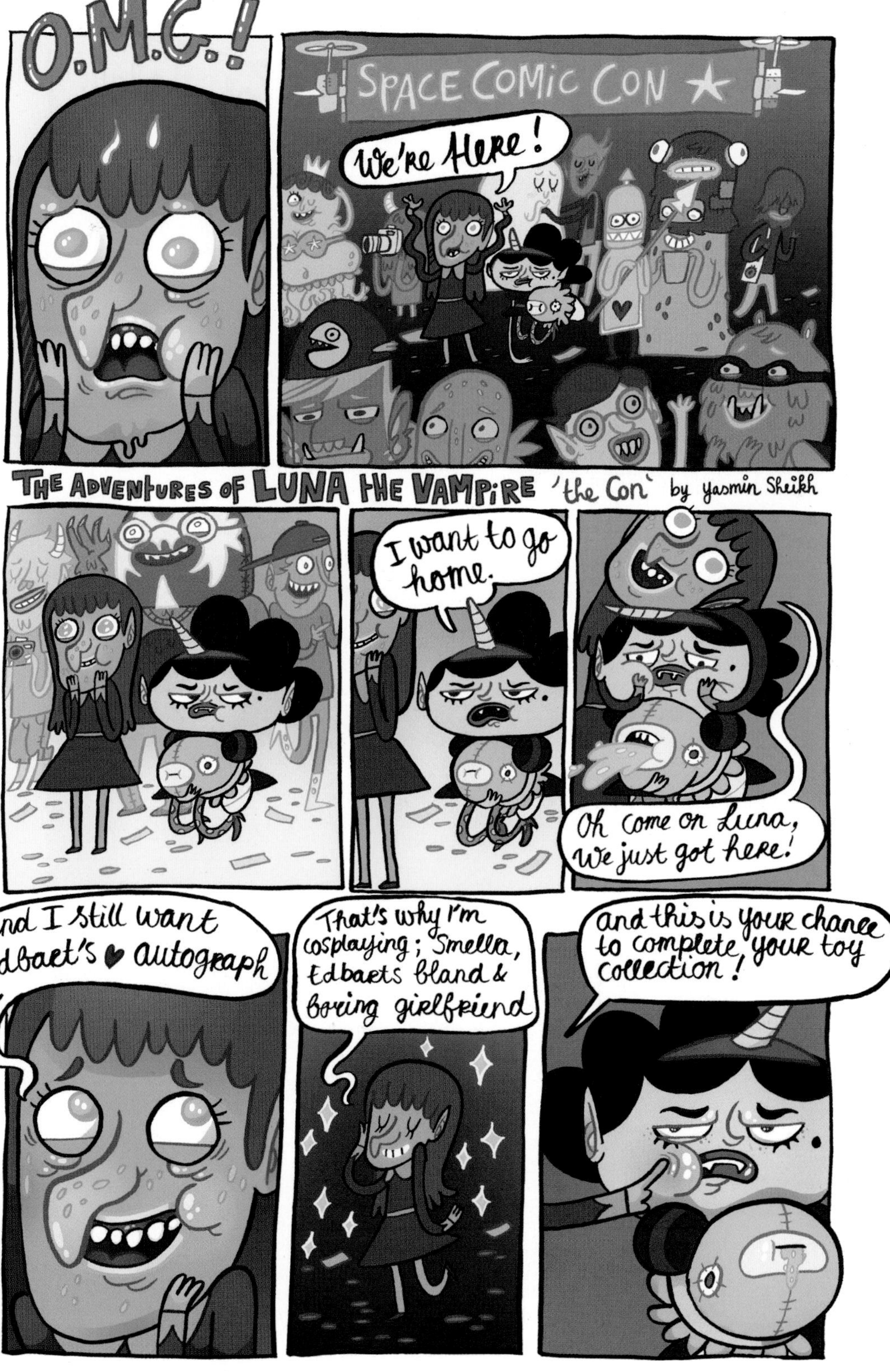

O.M.G.!
SPACE COMIC CON
We're Here!
THE ADVENTURES OF LUNA THE VAMPIRE 'the Con' by Yasmin Sheikh
I want to go home.
Oh come on Luna, we just got here!
nd I still want
dbart's ♥ autograph
That's why I'm cosplaying; Smella, Edbarts bland & boring girlfriend
and this is your chance to complete your toy collection!

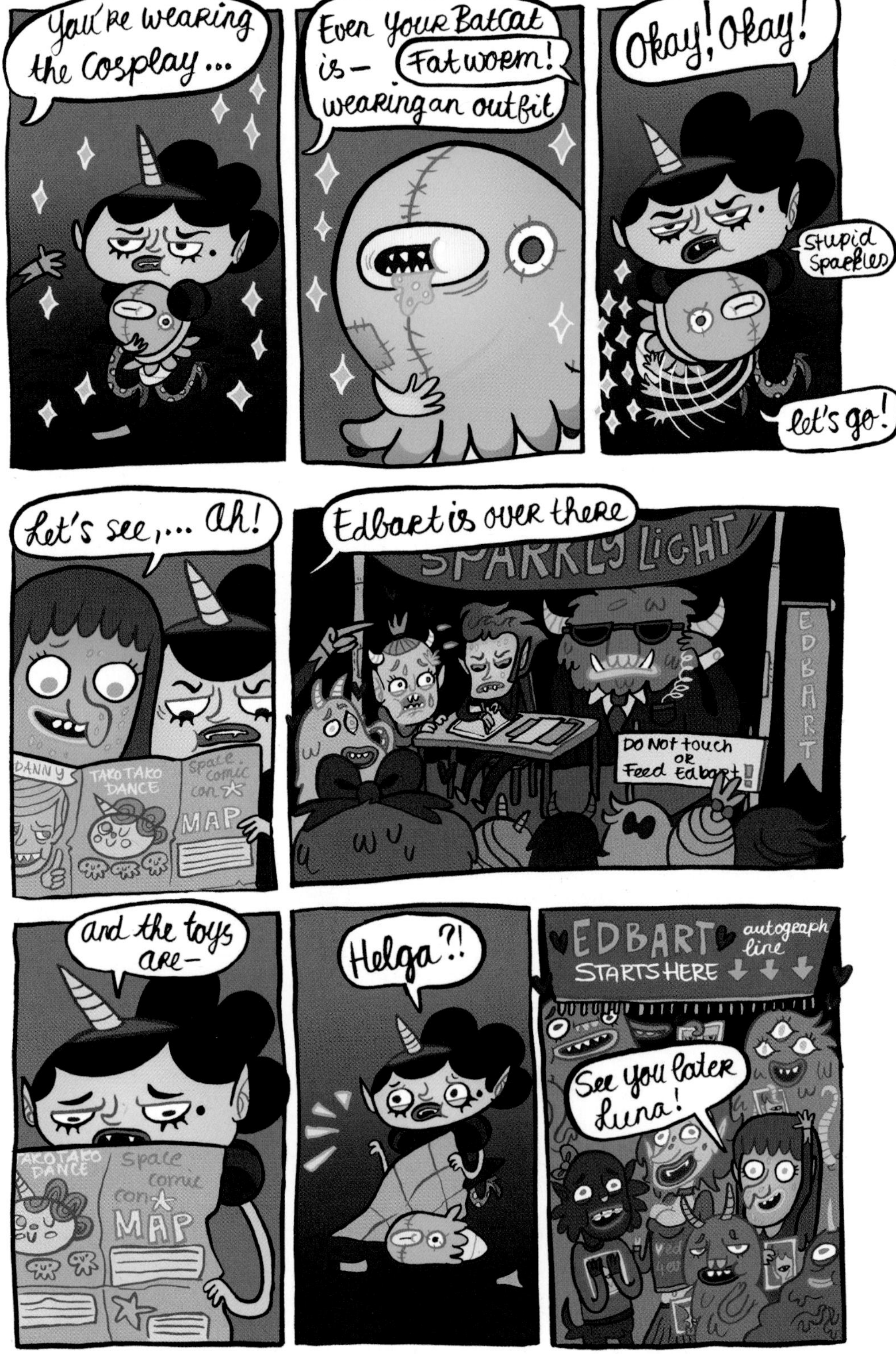
You're wearing the Cosplay...
Even your BatCat is–
Fatworm!
wearing an outfit
Okay! Okay!
Stupid Sparkles
let's go!
Let's see,... Ah!
DANNY
TAKO TAKO DANCE
Space comic con MAP
Edbart is over there
SPARKLY LIGHT
EDBART
DO NOT touch OR Feed Edbart!
and the toys are–
TAKO TAKO DANCE
Space comic con MAP
Helga?!
EDBART autograph line STARTS HERE
See you later Luna!

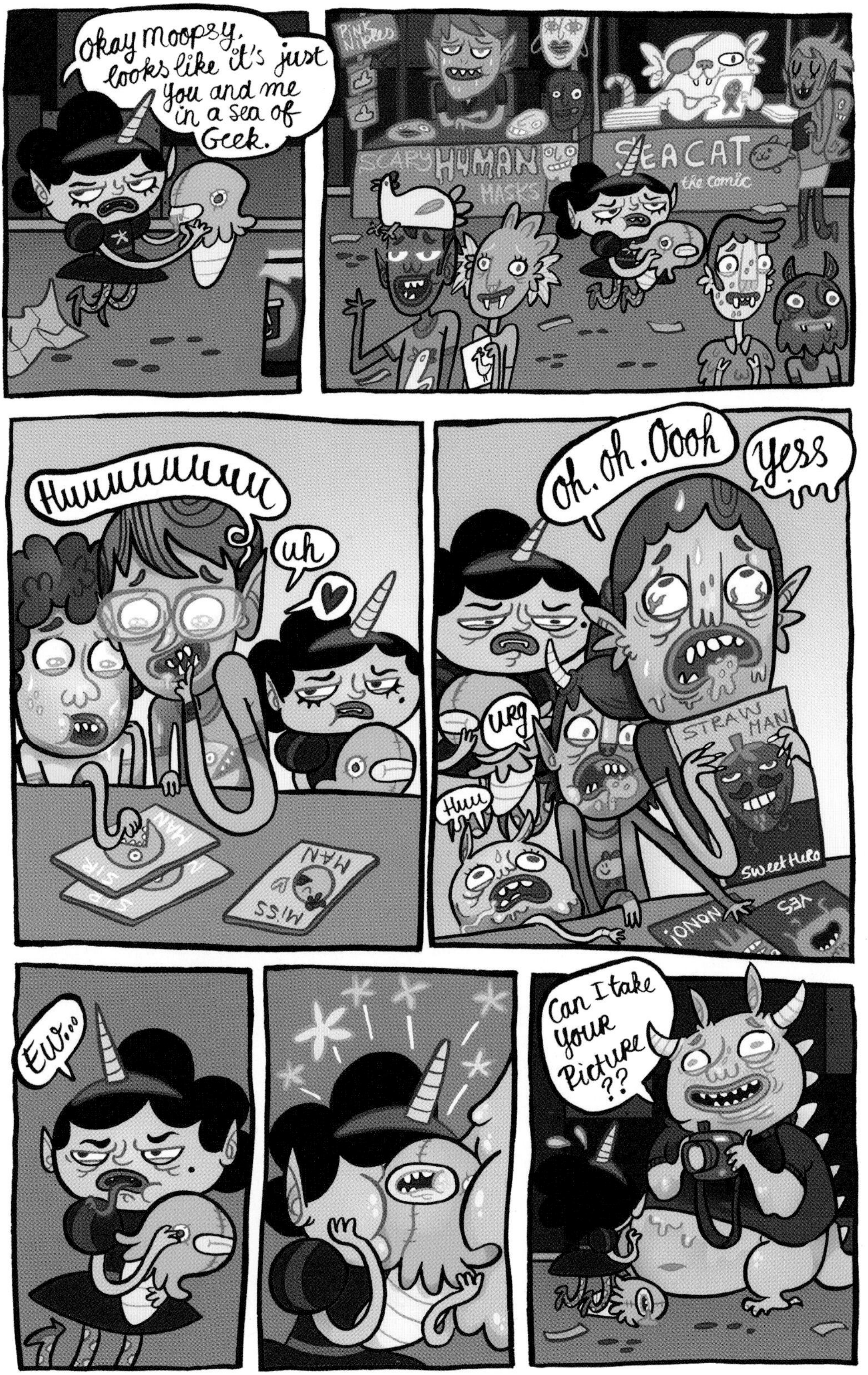
Okay moopsy, looks like it's just you and me in a sea of Geek.
PINK NIPPLES
SCARY HUMAN MASKS
SEACAT the comic
Huuuuuuuuu
uh
SIR MAN
MISS MAN
Oh. oh. Oooh
Yess
URG
Huu
STRAW MAN
Sweet Hero
NoNo!
YES
EW...
Can I take your Picture??

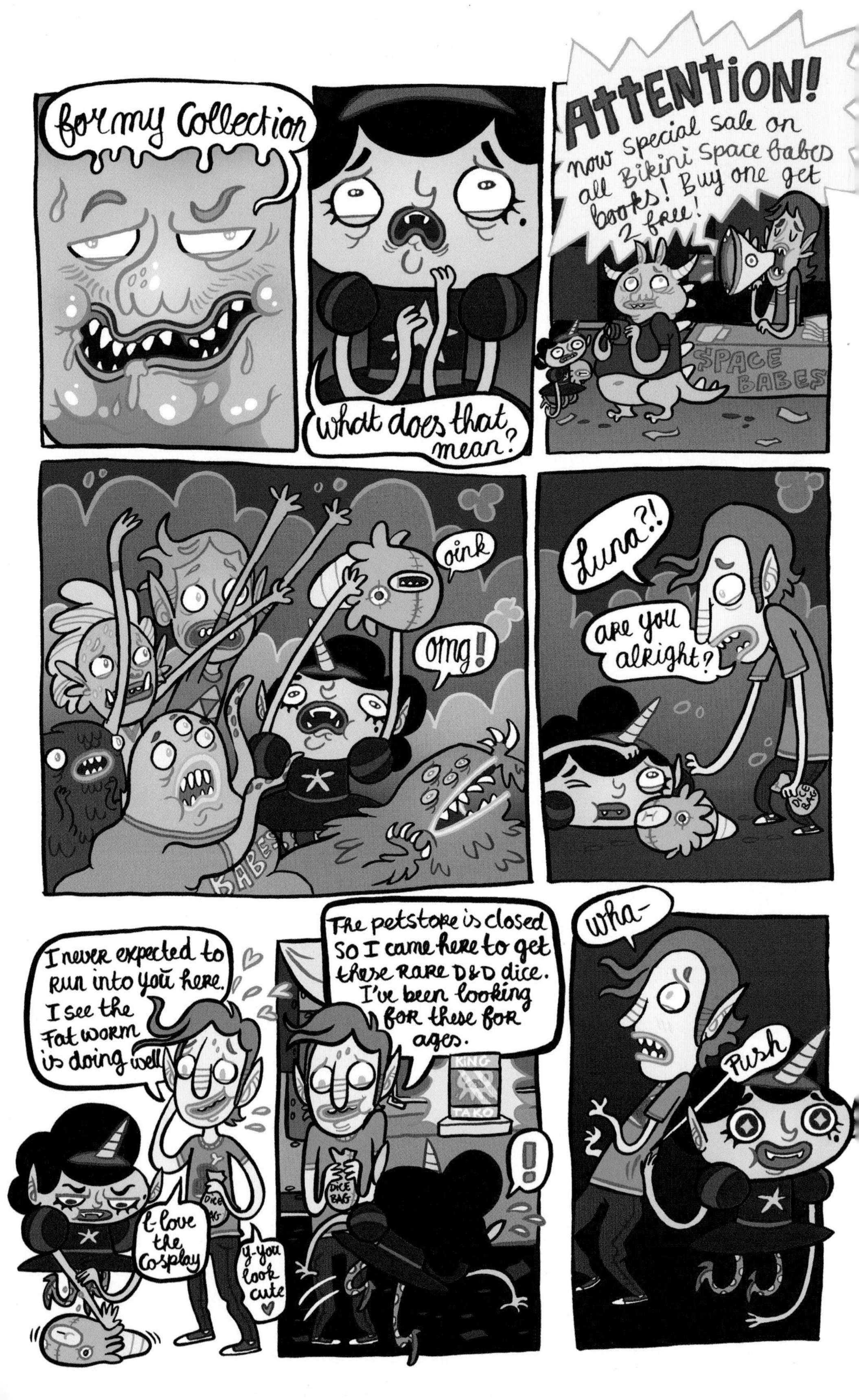

for my Collection
what does that mean?
ATTENTION!
now special sale on all Bikini Space Babes books! Buy one get 2 free!
SPACE BABES
oink
omg!
BABES
Luna?!
are you alright?
DICE BAG
I never expected to run into you here. I see the Fat worm is doing well
DICE BAG
I-love the Cosplay
y-you look cute
The petstore is closed so I came here to get these rare D&D dice. I've been looking for these for ages.
KING
TAKO
DICE BAG
!
wha-
Push

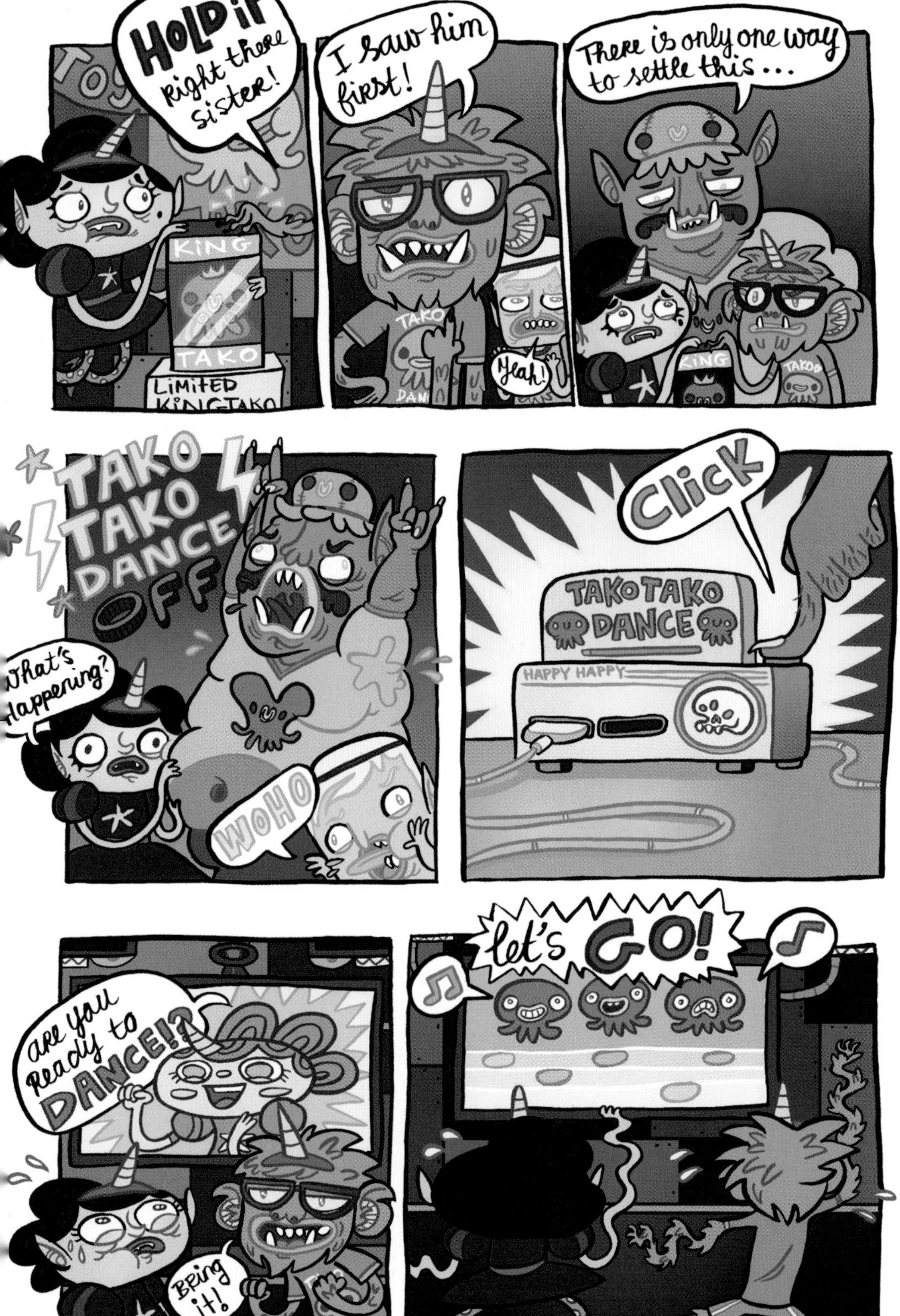
HOLD it right there sister!
TOY
KING
TAKO
LIMITED KING TAKO
I saw him first!
TAKO
Yeah!
There is only one way to settle this...
KING
TAKO
TAKO TAKO DANCE OFF
What's happening?
WOHO
CLICK
TAKO TAKO DANCE
HAPPY HAPPY
are you ready to DANCE!?
Bring it!
let's GO!

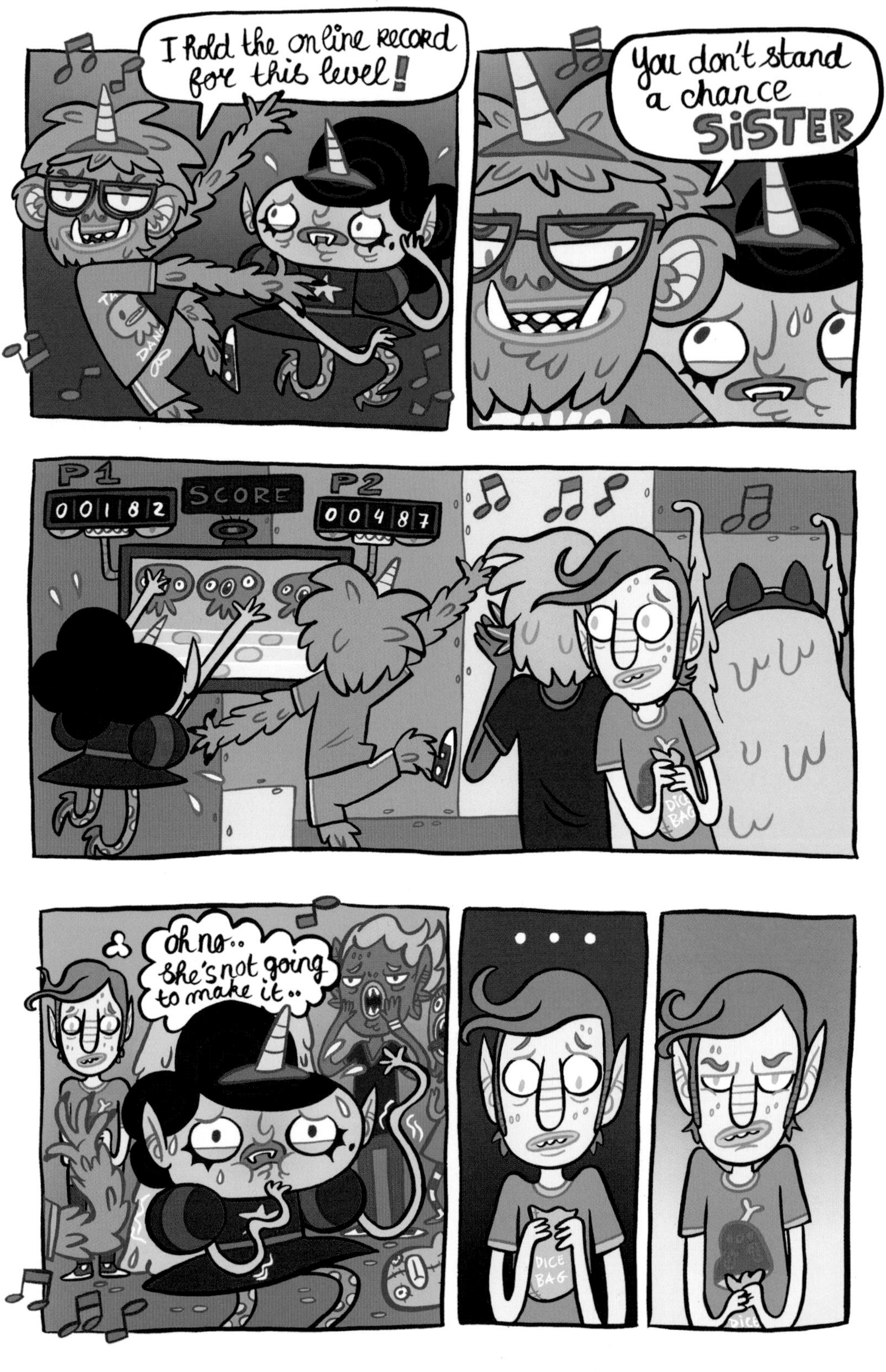
I hold the online record for this level!
You don't stand a chance SISTER
P1
00182
SCORE
P2
00487
DICE BAG
oh no.. She's not going to make it..
...
DICE BAG

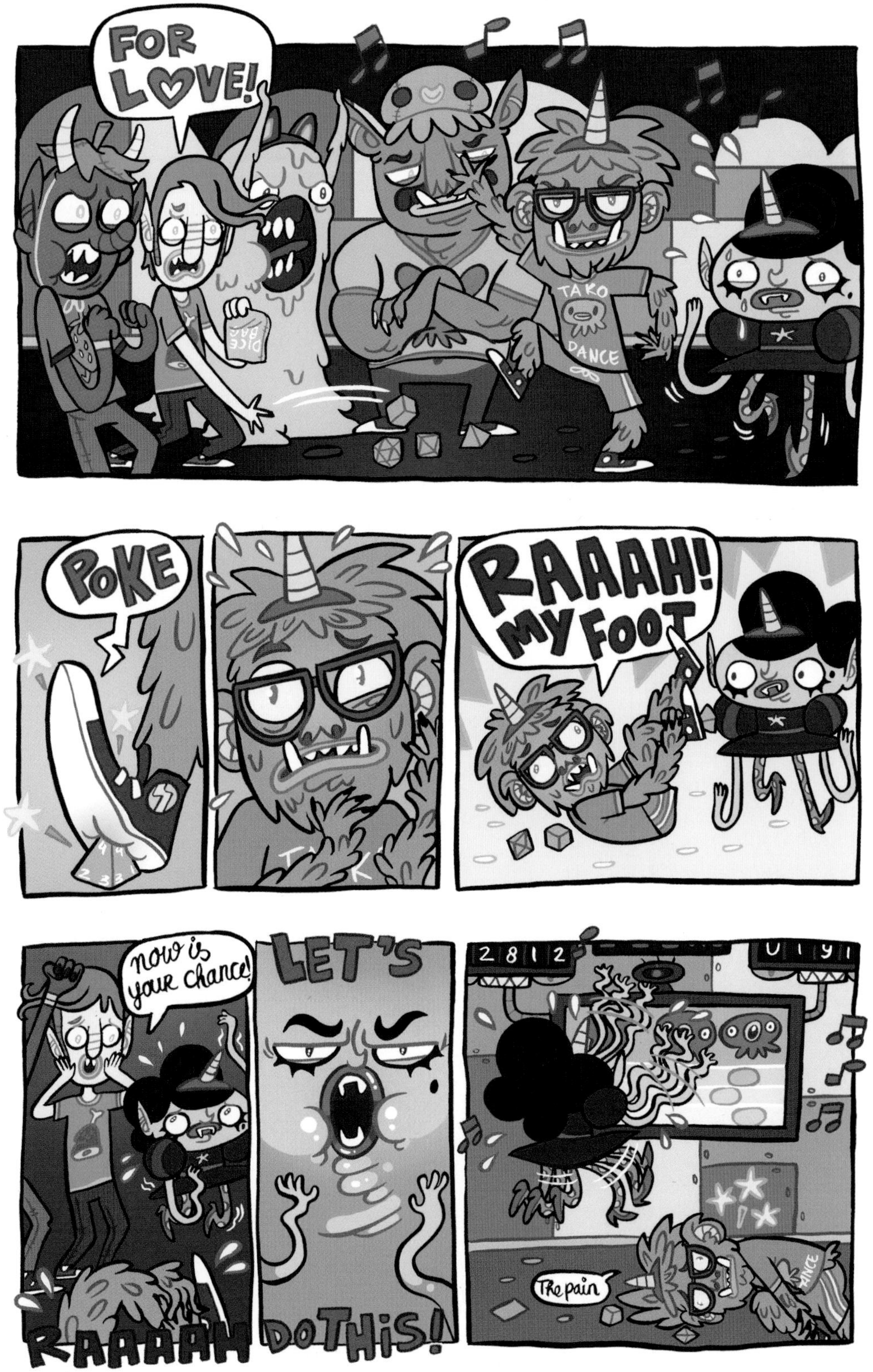
FOR LOVE!
TAKO DANCE
POKE
RAAAH! MY FOOT
now is your chance!
RAAAAH
LET'S DO THIS!
2812
The pain

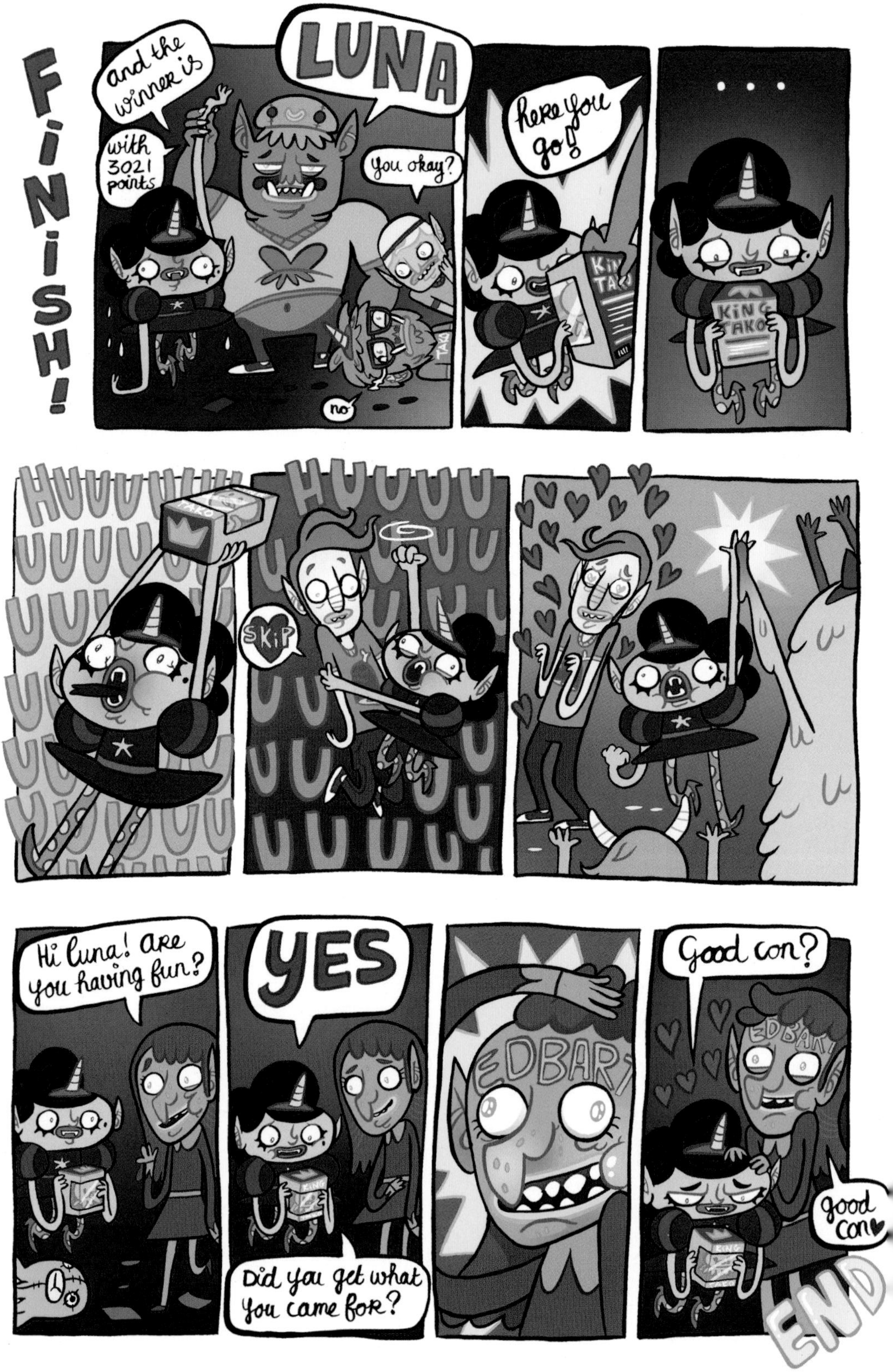
FINISH!
and the winner is
LUNA
with 3021 points
You okay?
no
here you go!
KING TAKO
...
KING TAKO
HUUUUUUUUUUUU
SKIP
HUUUUU
Hi luna! are you having fun?
YES
Did you get what you came for?
EDBART
Good con?
good con
END

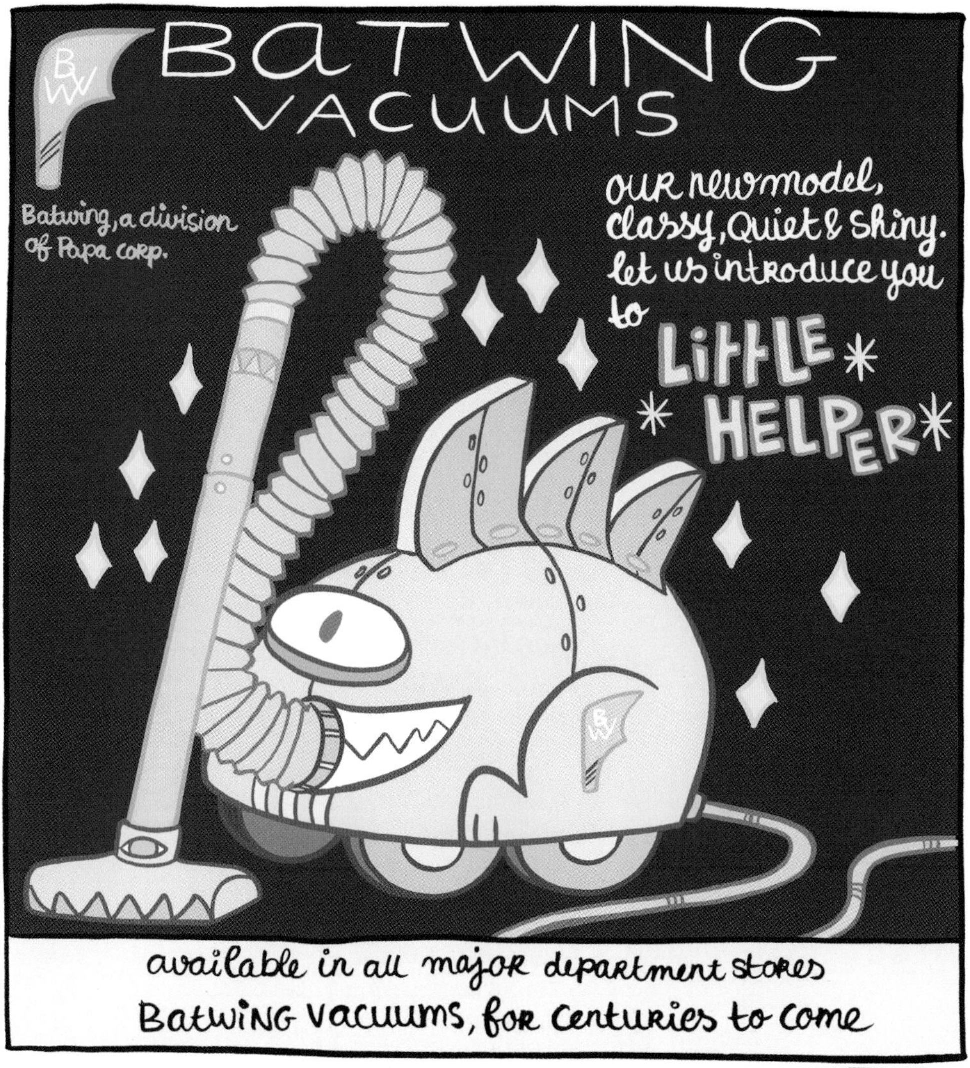

BW
BATWING
VACUUMS
Batwing, a division of Papa corp.
OUR new model, classy, Quiet & Shiny. let us introduce you to
LITTLE HELPER
BW
available in all major department stores
Batwing vacuums, for centuries to come

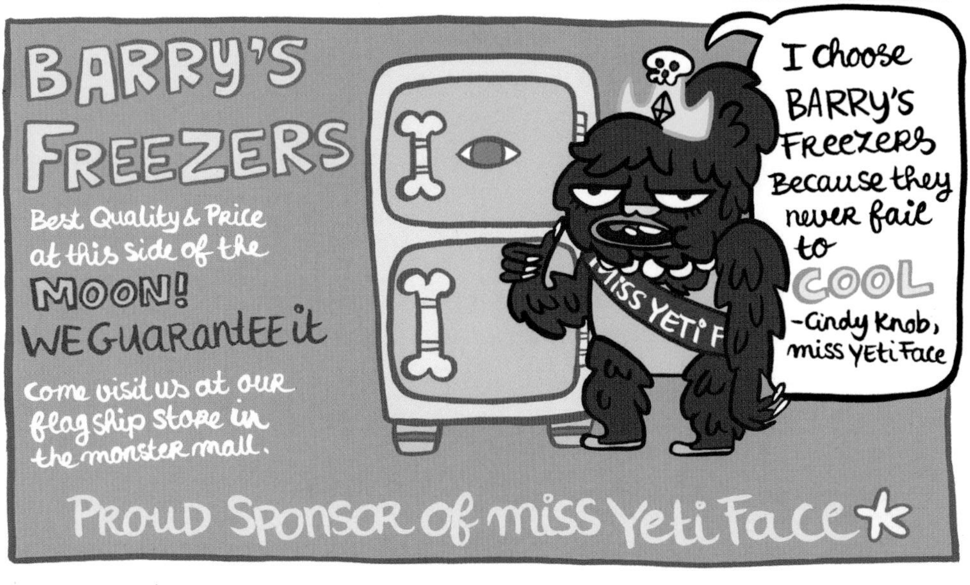

BARRY'S
FREEZERS
Best Quality & Price at this side of the
MOON!
WE GUARANTEE it
come visit us at our flagship store in the monster mall.
MISS YETI F
I choose BARRY'S FREEZERS Because they never fail to COOL -Cindy Knob, miss Yeti Face
PROUD SPONSOR of miss Yeti Face

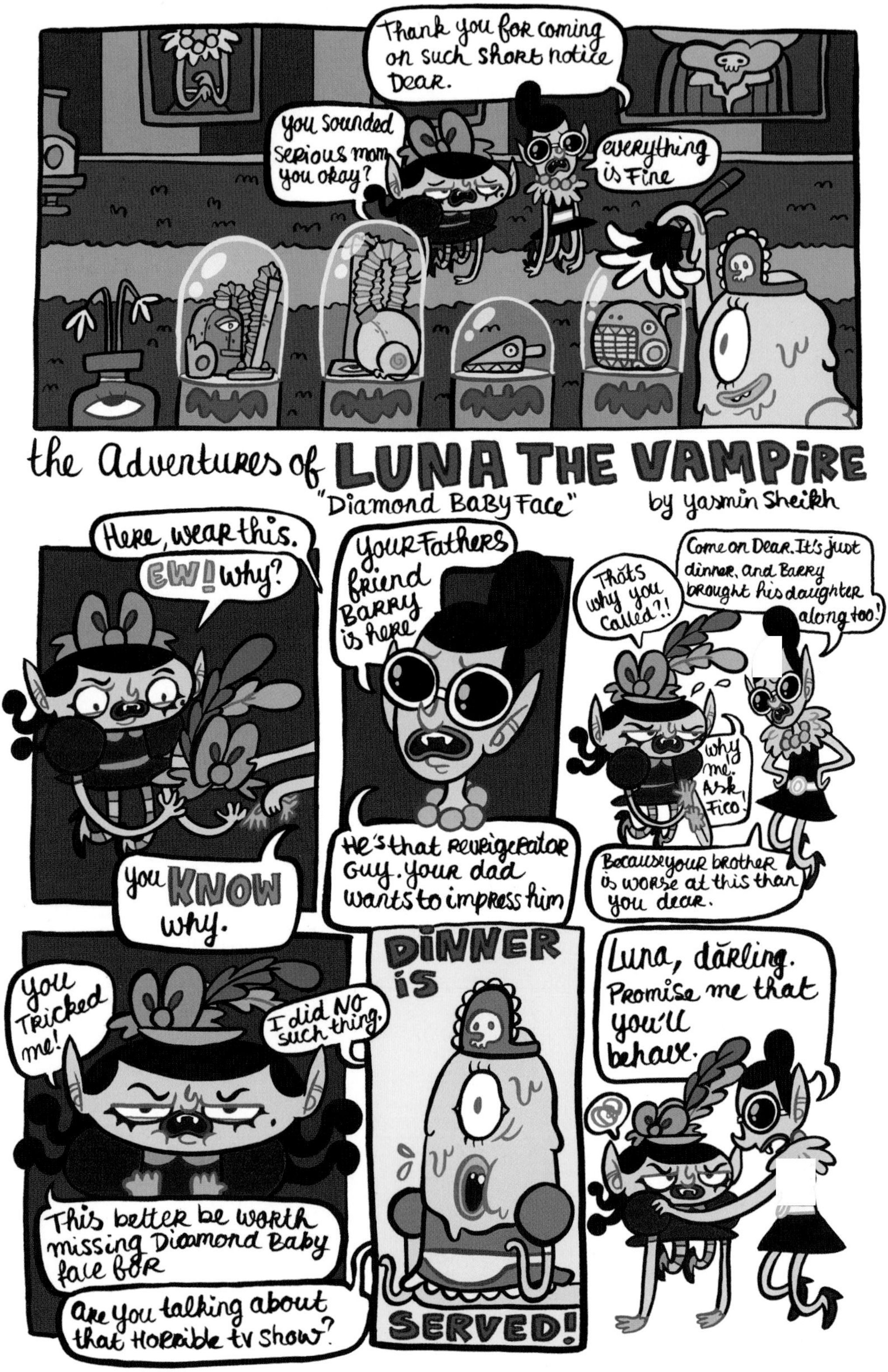

Thank you for coming on such short notice Dear.
you sounded serious mom you okay?
everything is Fine
the Adventures of LUNA THE VAMPIRE
"Diamond Baby Face"
by yasmin Sheikh
Here, wear this.
EW! why?
you KNOW why.
Your Fathers friend Barry is here
He's that refrigerator Guy. your dad wants to impress him
That's why you called?!
Come on Dear. It's just dinner, and Barry brought his daughter along too!
why me. Ask Fico!
Because your brother is worse at this than you dear.
You Tricked me!
I did NO such thing.
This better be worth missing Diamond Baby face for
Are you talking about that Horrible tv show?
DINNER IS SERVED!
Luna, darling. Promise me that you'll behave.

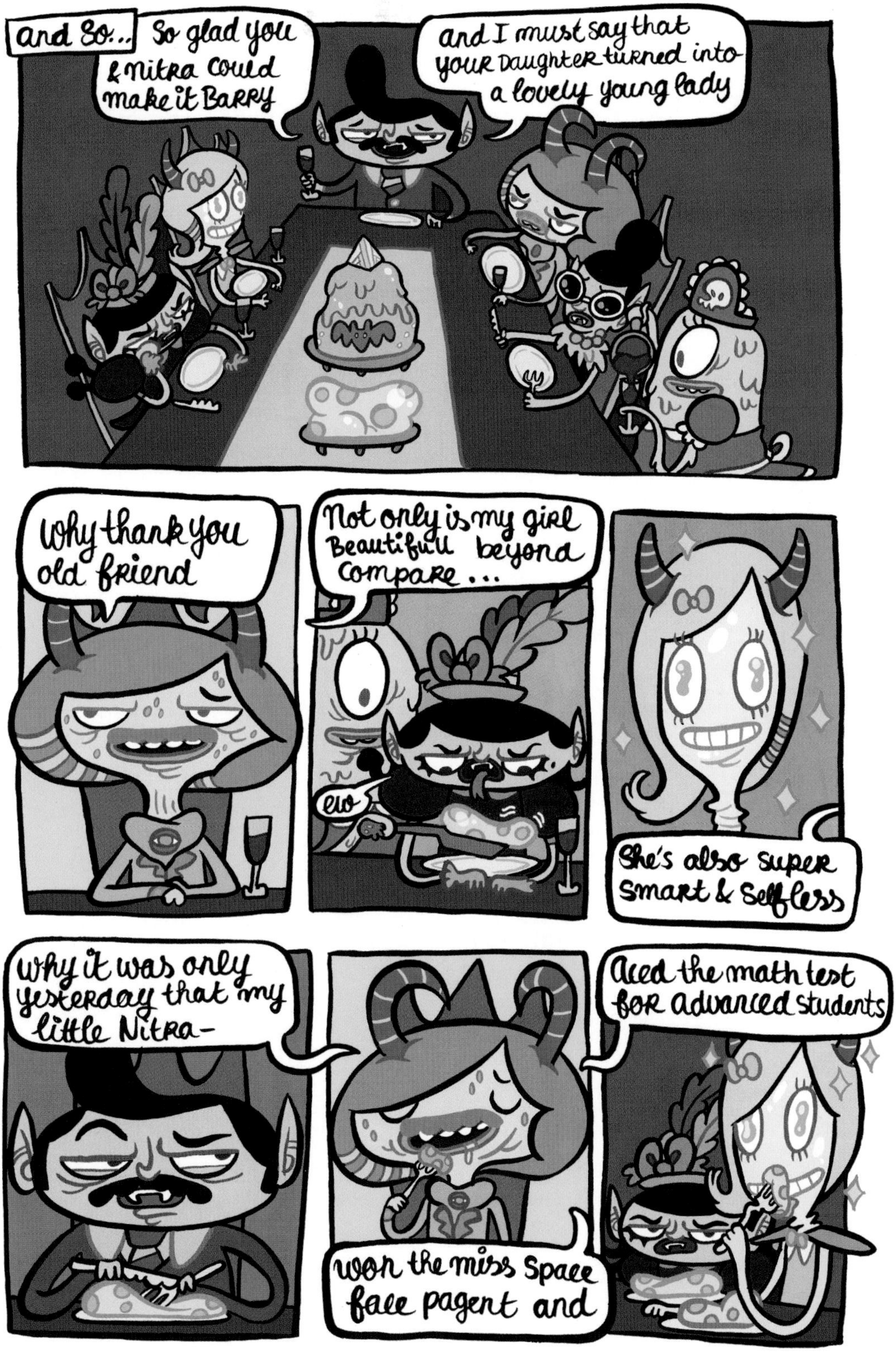
and So...
So glad you & Nitra could make it Barry
and I must say that your Daughter turned into a lovely young lady
Why thank you old friend
Not only is my girl Beautifull beyond compare...
ew
She's also super smart & Selfless
Why it was only yesterday that my little Nitra-
won the miss space face pagent and
Aced the math test for advanced students

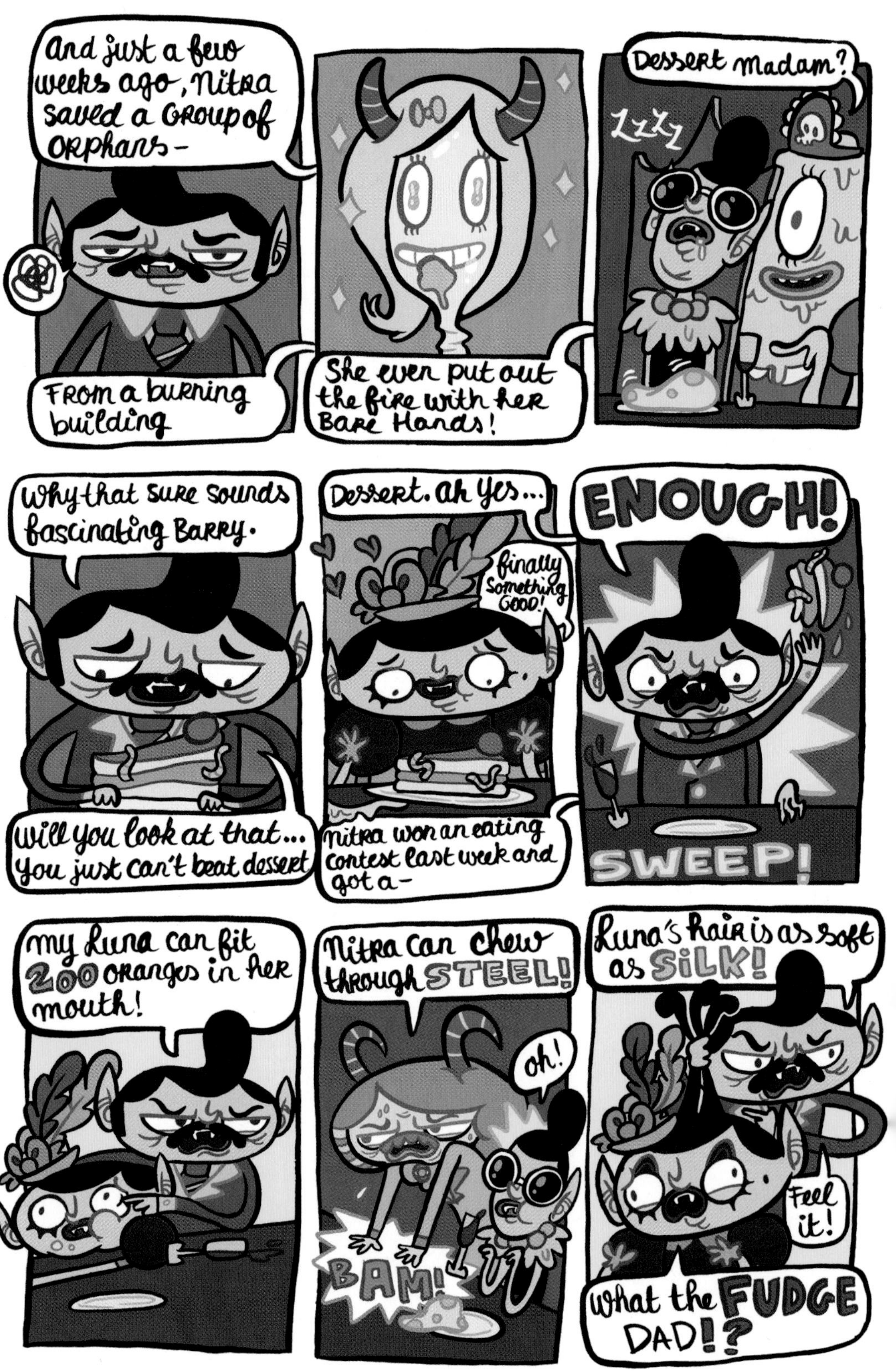
And just a few weeks ago, Nitra saved a group of orphans-
From a burning building
She even put out the fire with her Bare Hands!
Dessert Madam?
ZzZz
Why that sure sounds fascinating Barry.
Will you look at that... You just can't beat dessert
Dessert. ah yes...
finally something good!
Nitra won an eating contest last week and got a-
ENOUGH!
SWEEP!
My Luna can fit 200 oranges in her mouth!
Nitra can chew through STEEL!
oh!
BAM!
Luna's hair is as soft as SILK!
Feel it!
What the FUDGE DAD!?

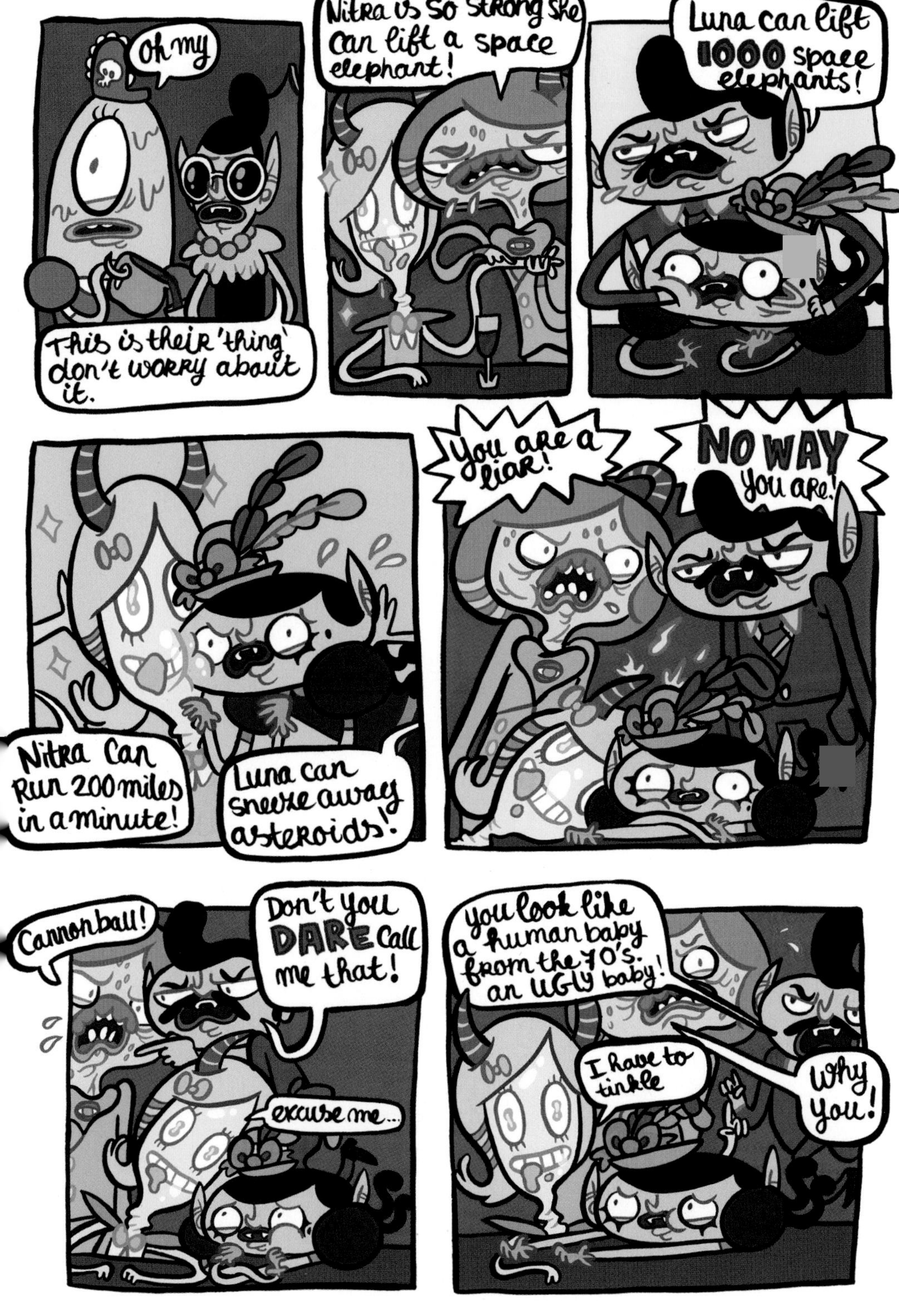
Oh my
This is their 'thing' don't worry about it.
Nitra is so strong she can lift a space elephant!
Luna can lift 1000 space elephants!
Nitra Can Run 200 miles in a minute!
Luna can sneeze away asteroids!
You are a liar!
NO WAY You are!
Cannonball!
Don't you DARE call me that!
excuse me...
You look like a human baby from the 70's. an UGLY baby!
I have to tinkle
Why You!

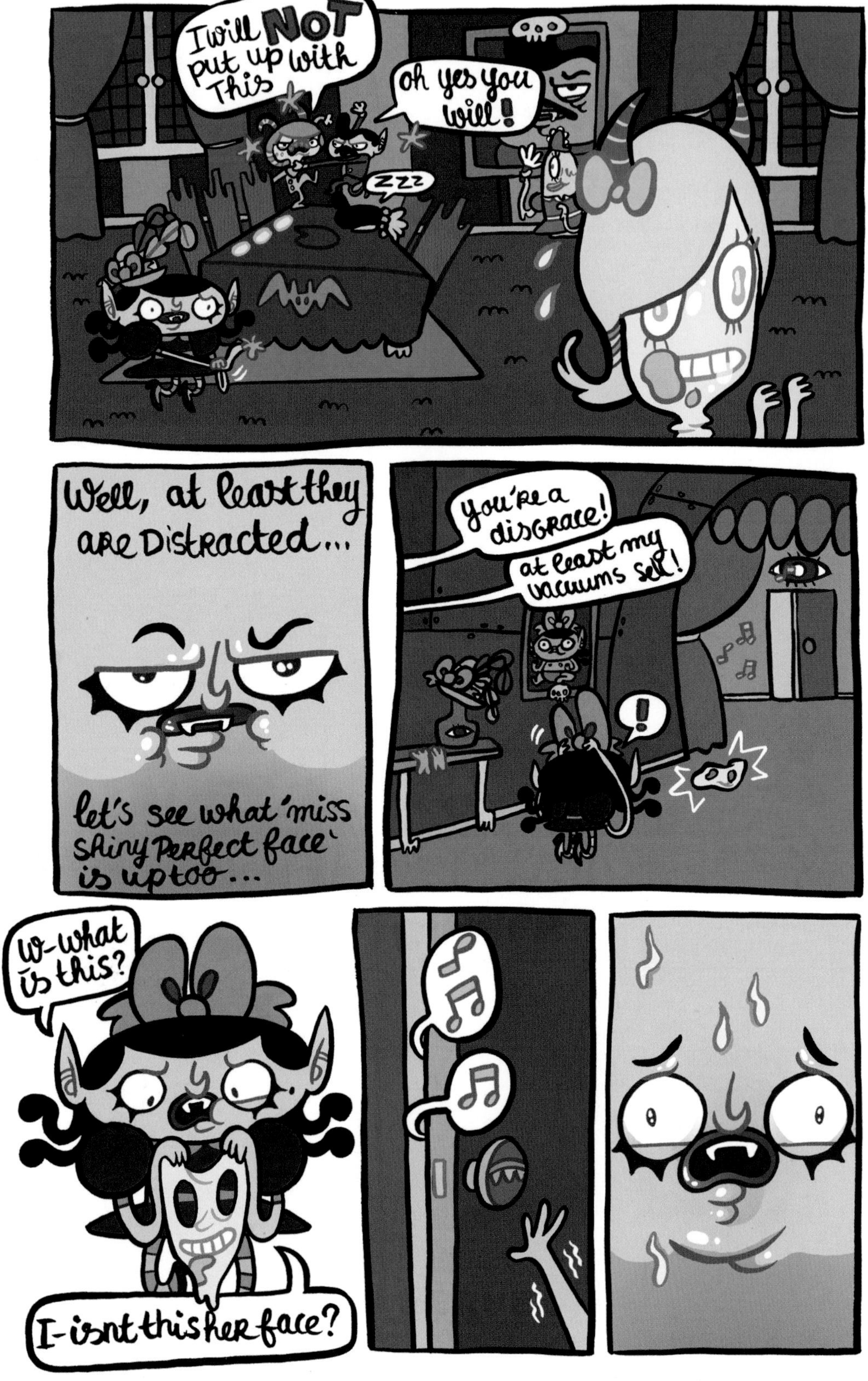
I will NOT put up with This
oh yes you will!
ZZZ
Well, at least they are Distracted...
let's see what 'miss shiny Perfect face' is up too...
You're a disgrace!
at least my vacuums sell!
!
W-what is this?
I-isnt this her face?

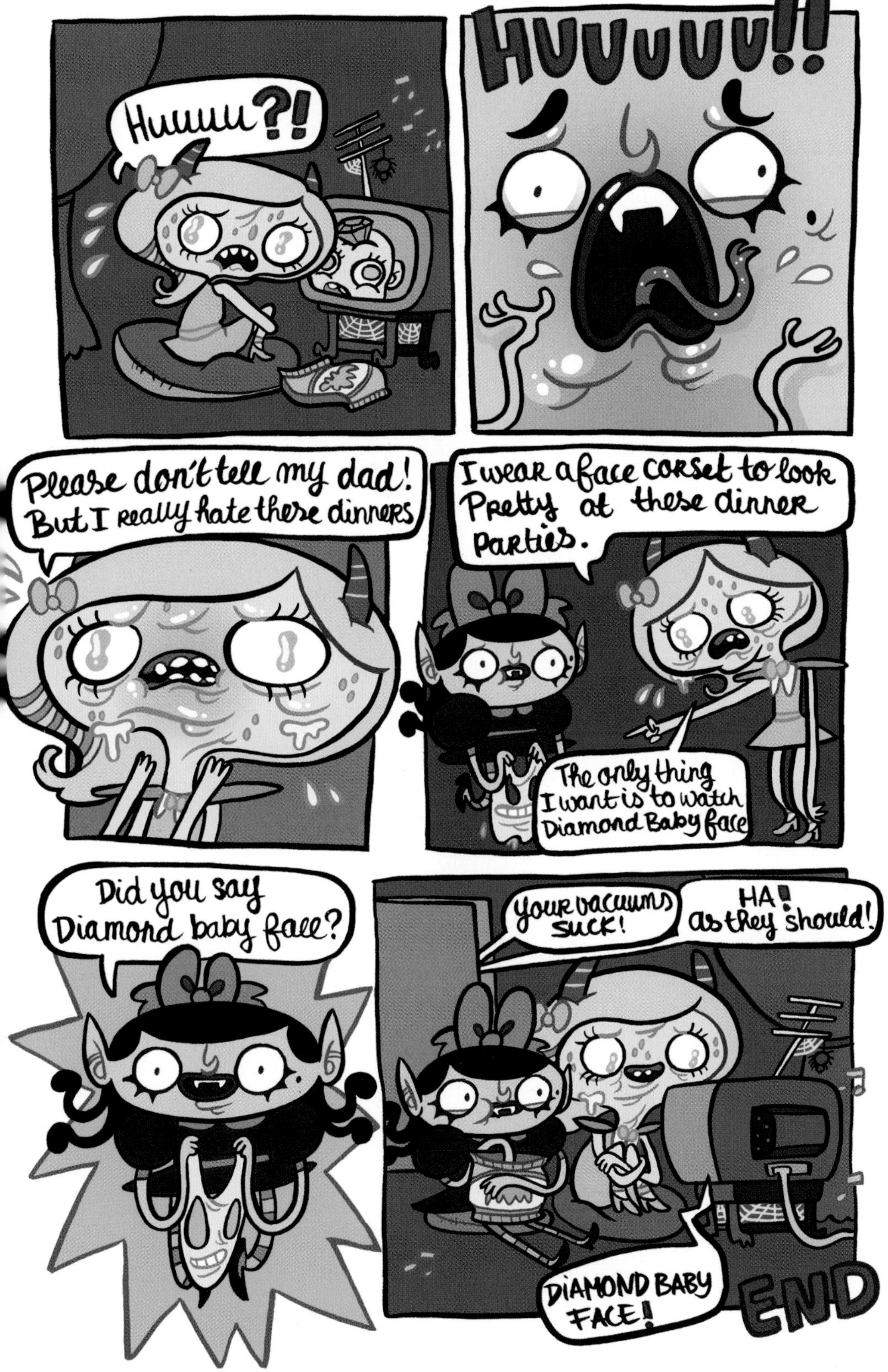
Huuuuu?!
HUUUUUU!!
Please don't tell my dad! But I really hate these dinners
I wear a face corset to look Pretty at these dinner parties.
The only thing I want is to watch Diamond Baby face
Did you say Diamond baby face?
Your vacuums suck!
HA! as they should!
DIAMOND BABY FACE!
END

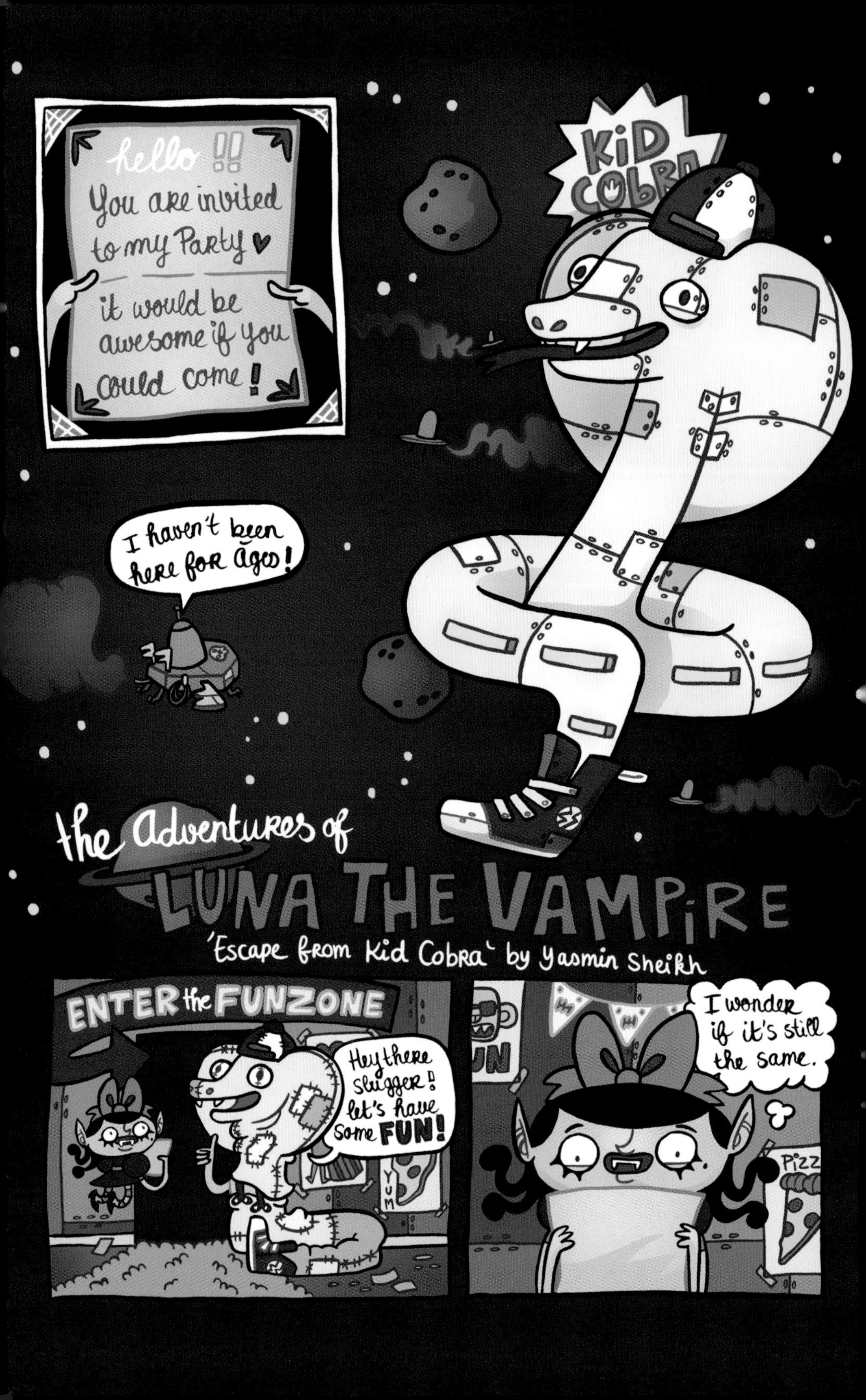
hello !!
You are invited to my Party
it would be awesome if you could come!
KID COBRA
I haven't been here for ages!
the Adventures of
LUNA THE VAMPIRE
'Escape from Kid Cobra' by Yasmin Sheikh
ENTER the FUNZONE
Hey there slugger! let's have some FUN!
YUM
I wonder if it's still the same.
PIZZ

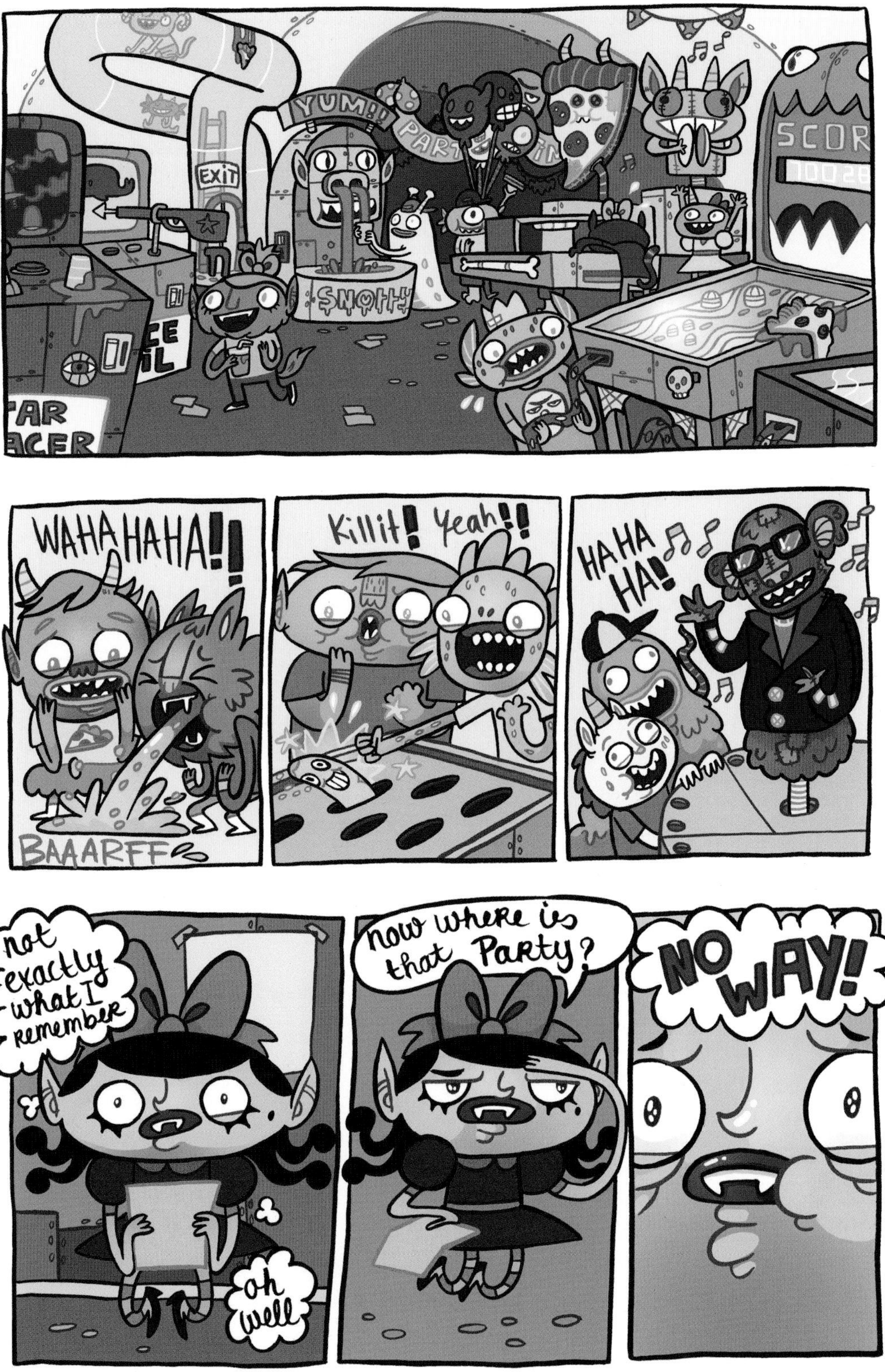
YUM!!
EXIT
WAHAHAHA!!
BAAARFF
Killit! Yeah!!
HAHA HA!
not exactly what I remember
oh well
now where is that Party?
NO WAY!

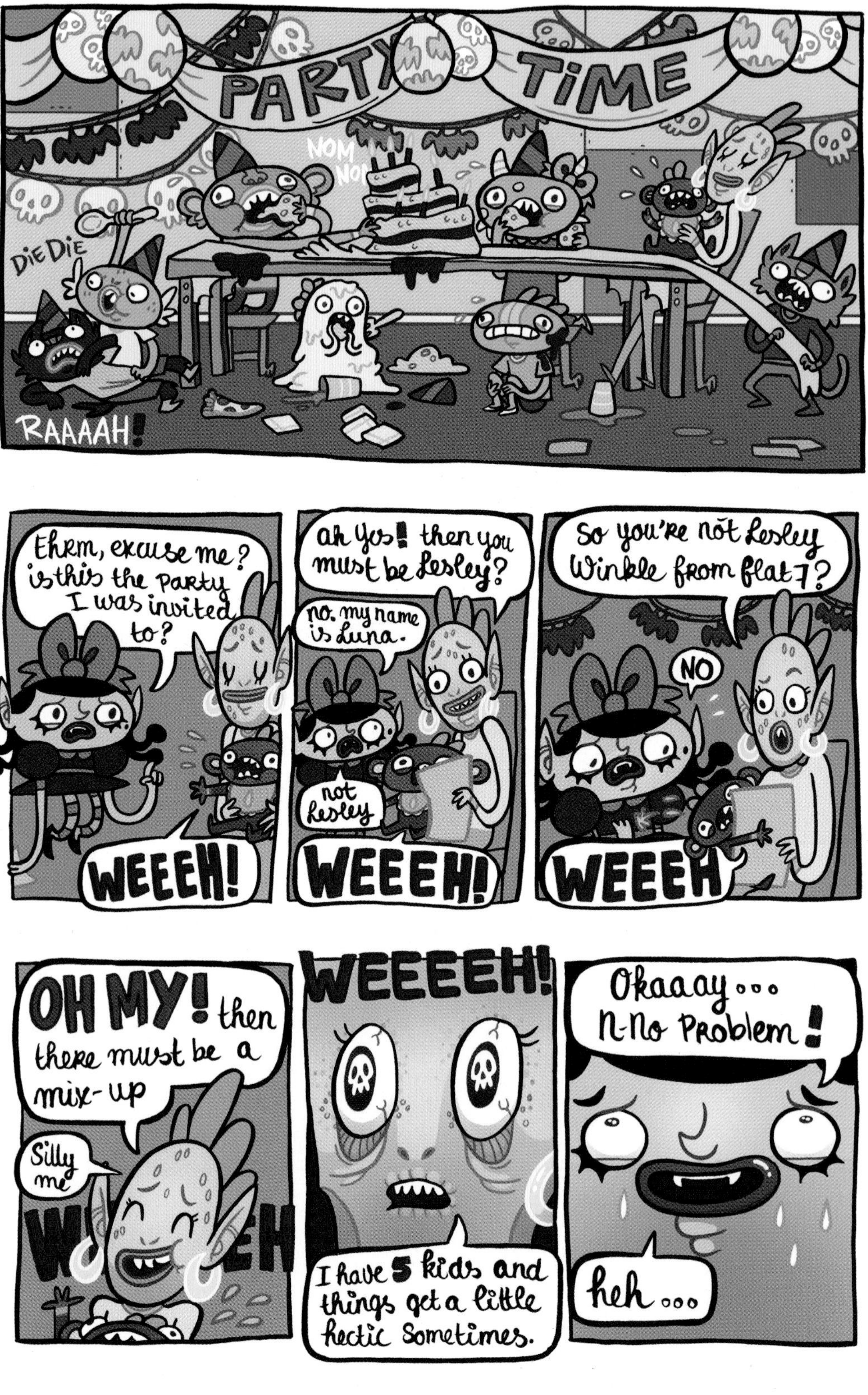
PARTY TIME
NOM NOM
DIE DIE
RAAAAH!
Ehrm, excuse me? is this the party I was invited to?
WEEEH!
ah Yes! then you must be Lesley?
no, my name is Luna.
not Lesley
WEEEH!
So you're not Lesley Winkle from flat 7?
NO
WEEEH
OH MY! then there must be a mix-up
Silly me
WEEEEH!
I have 5 kids and things get a little hectic Sometimes.
Okaaay...
N-No Problem!
heh...

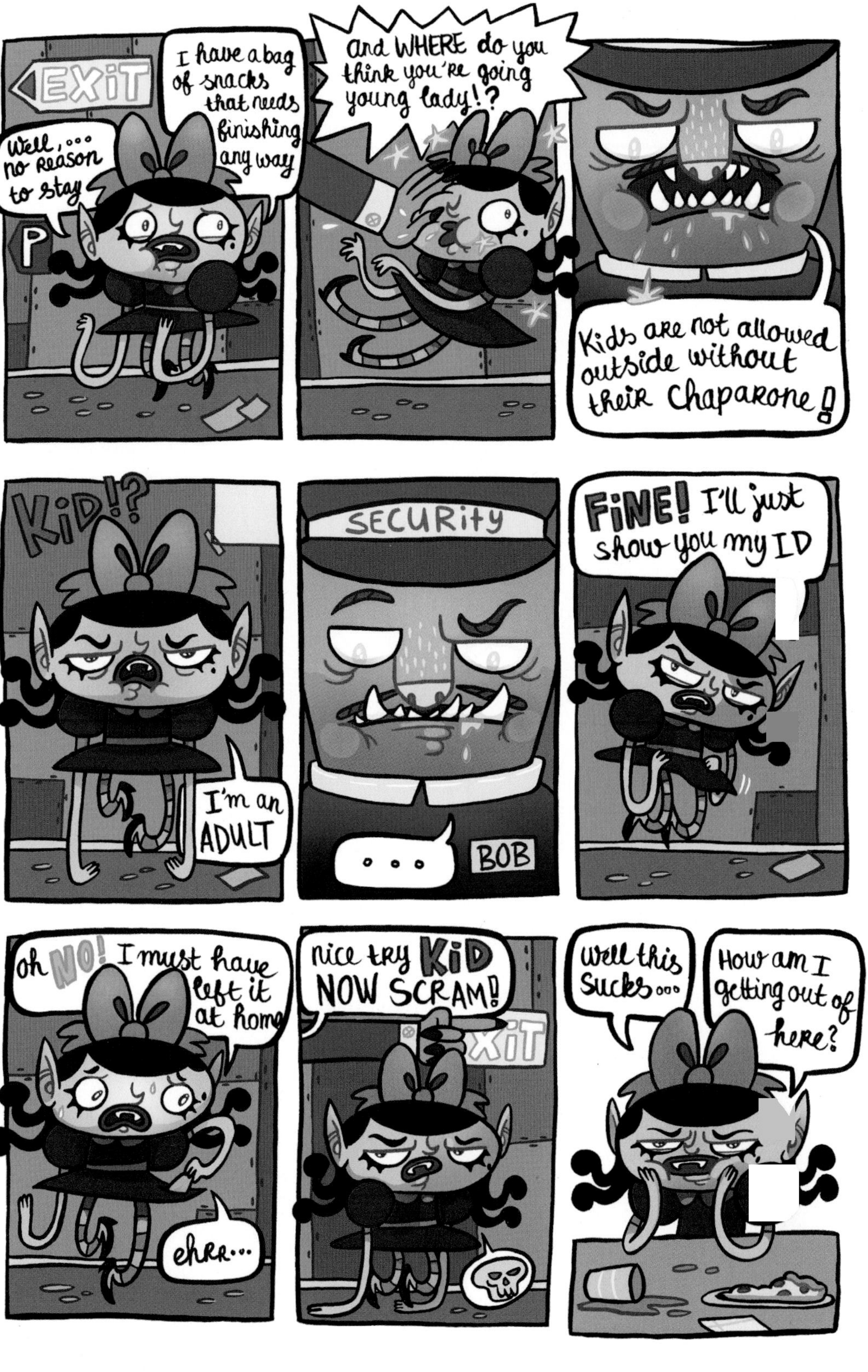
EXIT
Well,... no Reason to stay
I have a bag of snacks that needs finishing any way
P
and WHERE do you think you're going young lady!?
Kids are not allowed outside without their Chaparone!
KiD!?
I'm an ADULT
SECURity
...
BOB
FiNE! I'll just show you my ID
oh NO! I must have left it at home
ehRR...
nice try KiD NOW SCRAM!
XiT
Well this Sucks...
How am I getting out of here?

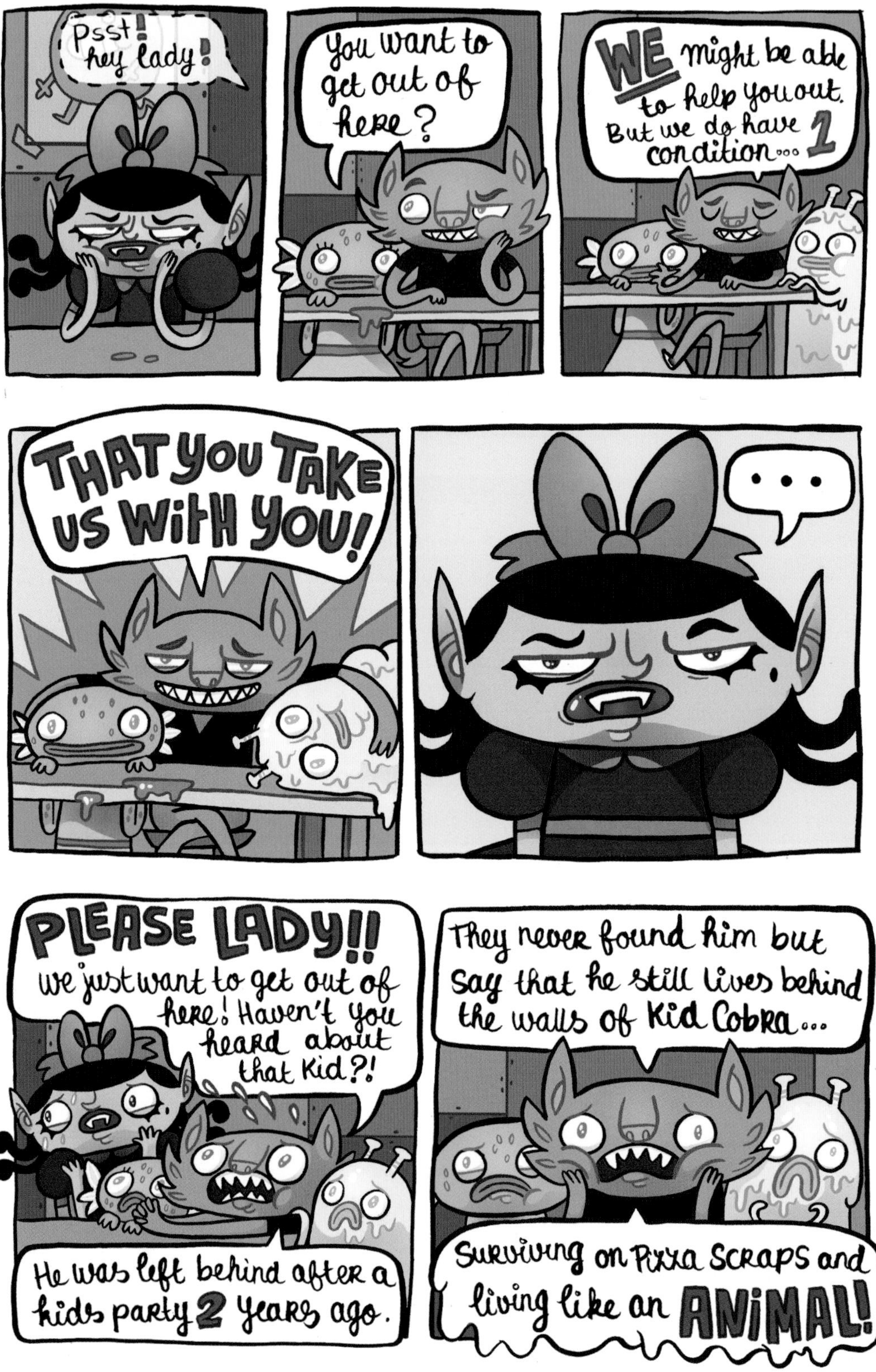
Psst! hey lady!
You want to get out of here?
WE might be able to help you out. But we do have 1 condition...
THAT YOU TAKE US WITH YOU!
...
PLEASE LADY!! we just want to get out of here! Haven't you heard about that Kid?!
He was left behind after a kids party 2 years ago.
They never found him but say that he still lives behind the walls of Kid Cobra...
Surviving on Pizza scraps and living like an ANIMAL!

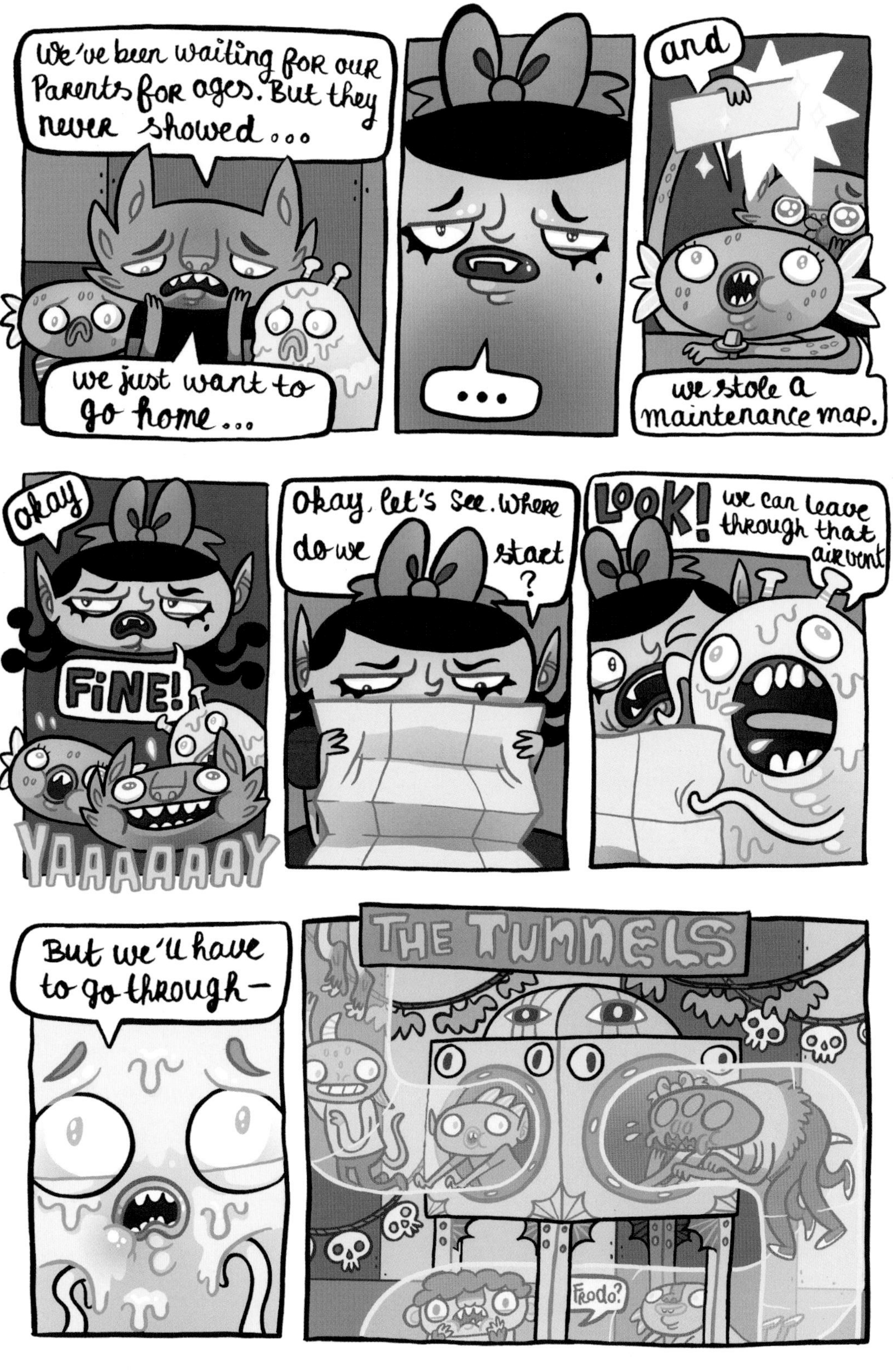

We've been waiting for our Parents for ages. But they never showed...
we just want to go home...
...
and
we stole a maintenance map.
okay
FiNE!
YAAAAAAY
Okay, let's see. Where do we start?
LOOK! we can leave through that air vent
But we'll have to go through–
THE TUNNELS
Frodo?

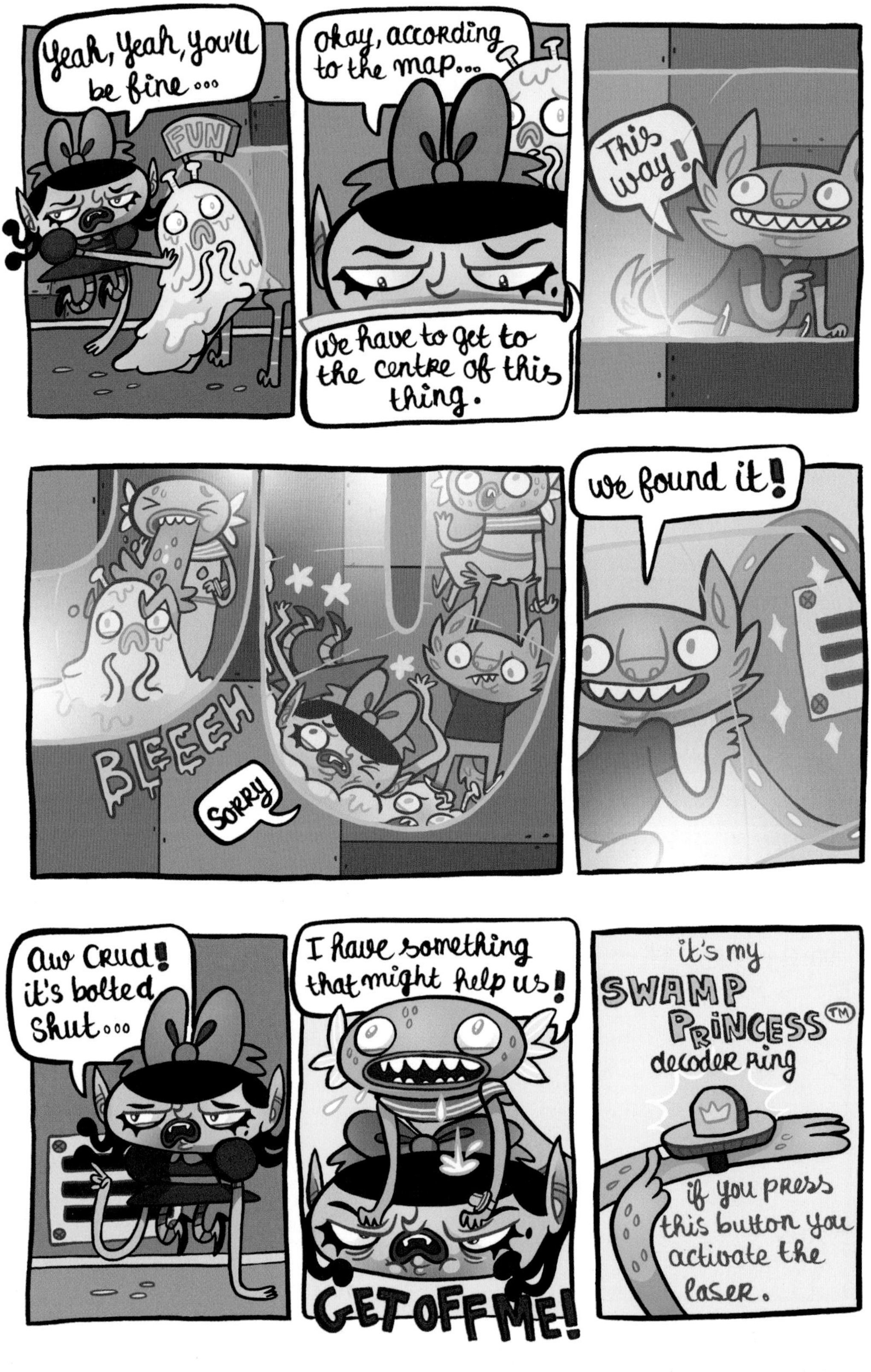

Yeah, Yeah, you'll be fine...
FUN
Okay, according to the map...
We have to get to the centre of this thing.
This way!
BLEEEH
SORRY
We found it!
Aw Crud! it's bolted Shut...
I have something that might help us!
GET OFF ME!
it's my SWAMP PRiNCESS™ decoder Ring
if you press this button you activate the laser.

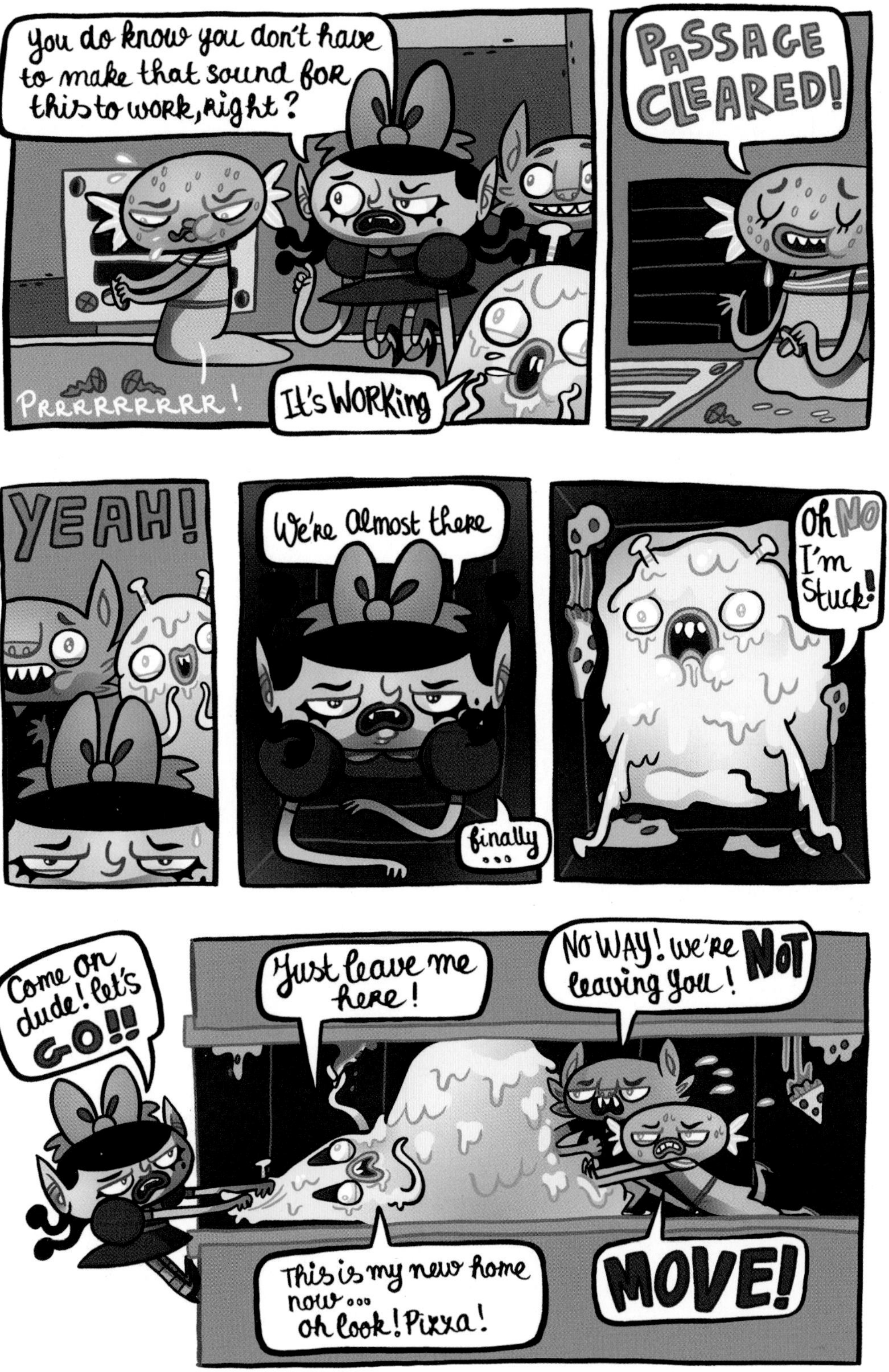
You do know you don't have to make that sound for this to work, right?
Prrrrrrrrr!
It's WORKing
PASSAGE CLEARED!
YEAH!
We're almost there
finally ...
Oh NO I'm Stuck!
Come on dude! let's GO!!
Just leave me here!
NO WAY! we're NOT leaving you!
This is my new home now... oh look! Pizza!
MOVE!

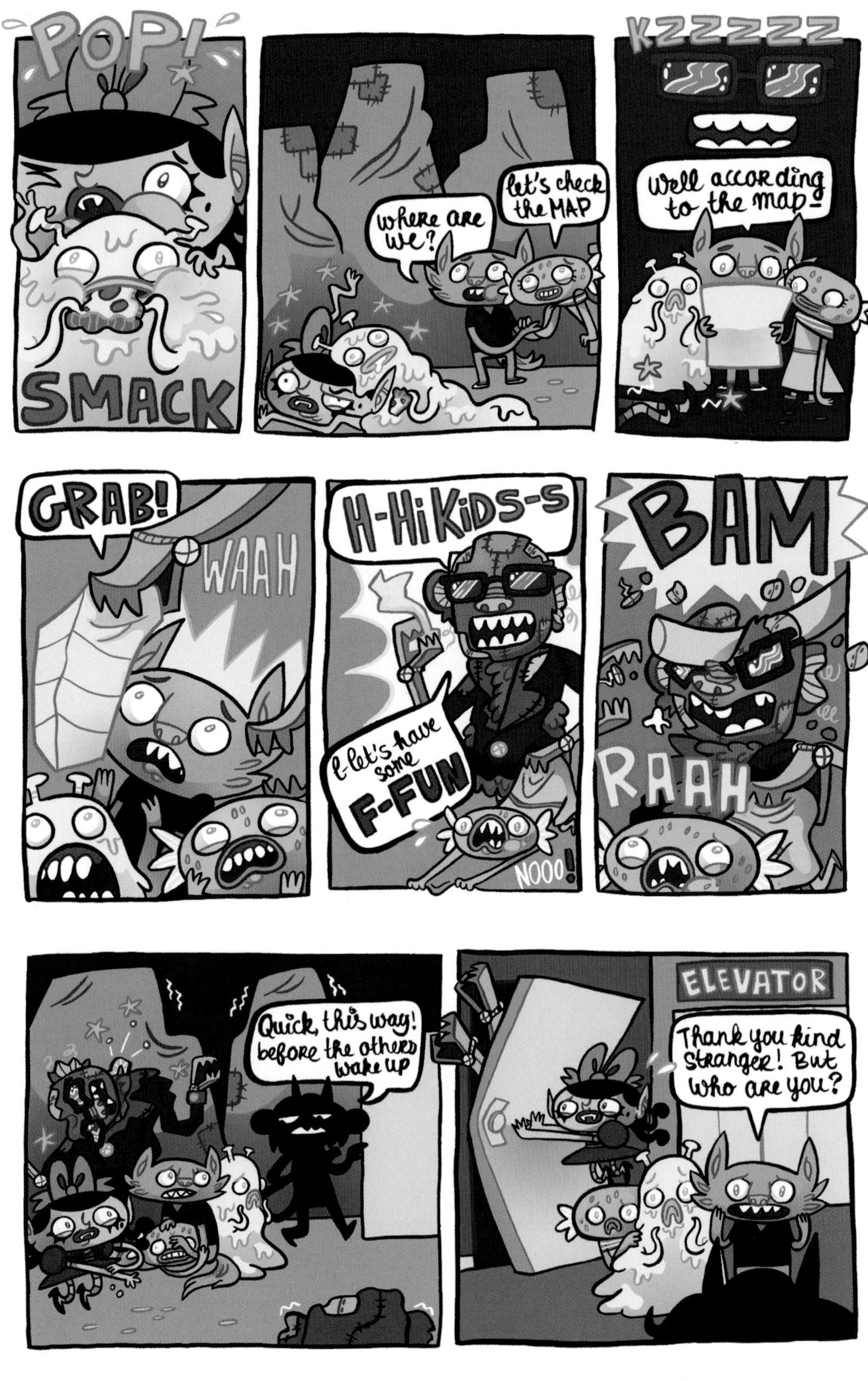
POP!
SMACK
where are we?
let's check the MAP
KZZZZZ
Well according to the map-
GRAB!
WAAH
H-Hi KiDS-S
l-let's have some F-FUN
NOOO!
BAM
RAAH
Quick, this way! before the others wake up
ELEVATOR
Thank you kind stranger! But who are you?

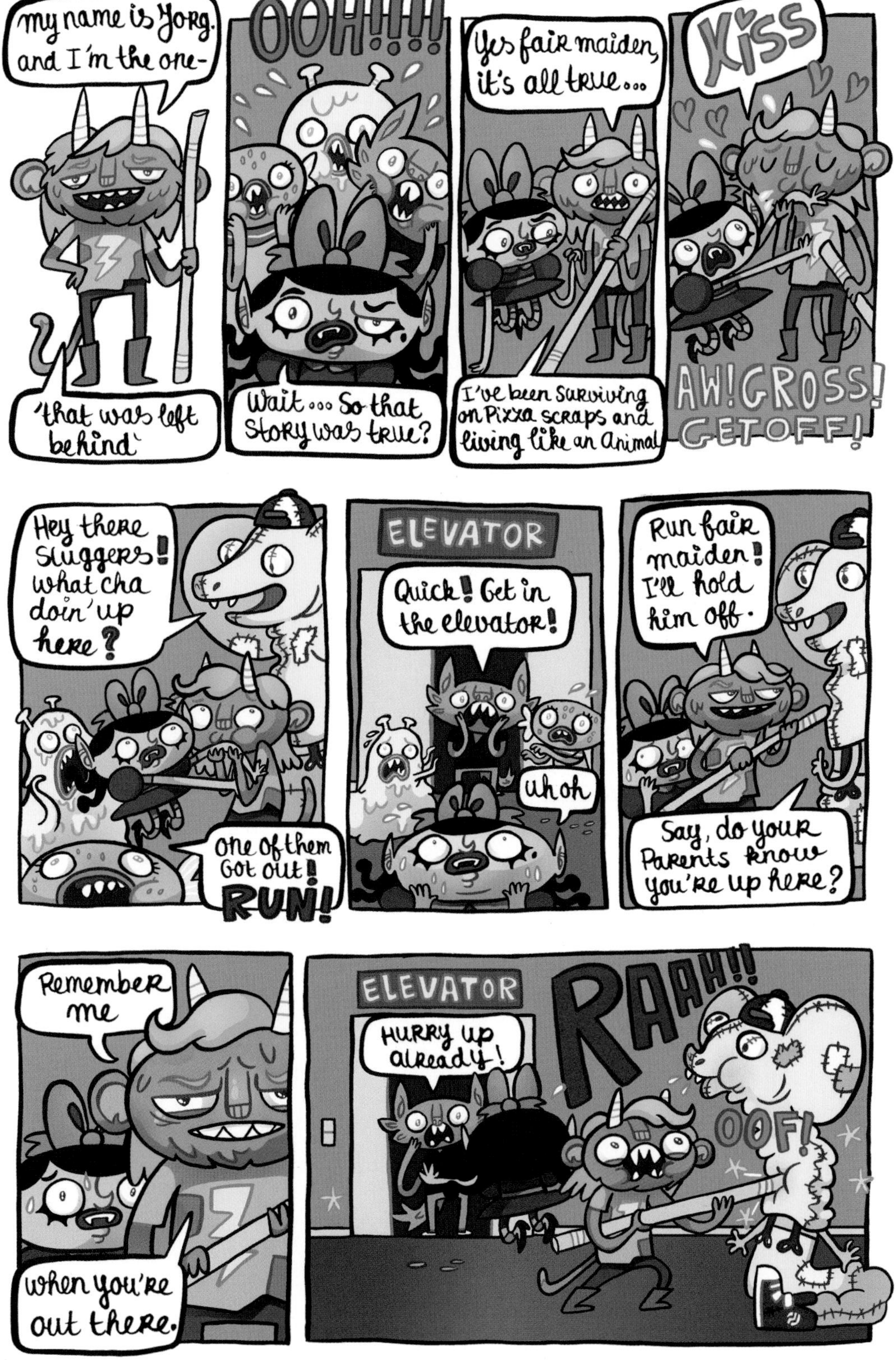

my name is Yorg. and I'm the one-
'that was left behind'
OOH!!!!
Wait... So that story was true?
Yes fair maiden, it's all true...
I've been surviving on Pizza scraps and living like an animal
KISS
AW! GROSS! GET OFF!
Hey there sluggers! what cha doin' up here?
One of them Got out! RUN!
ELEVATOR
Quick! Get in the elevator!
uh oh
Run fair maiden! I'll hold him off.
Say, do your Parents know you're up here?
Remember me
when you're out there.
ELEVATOR
RAAH!!
HURRY up already!
OOF!

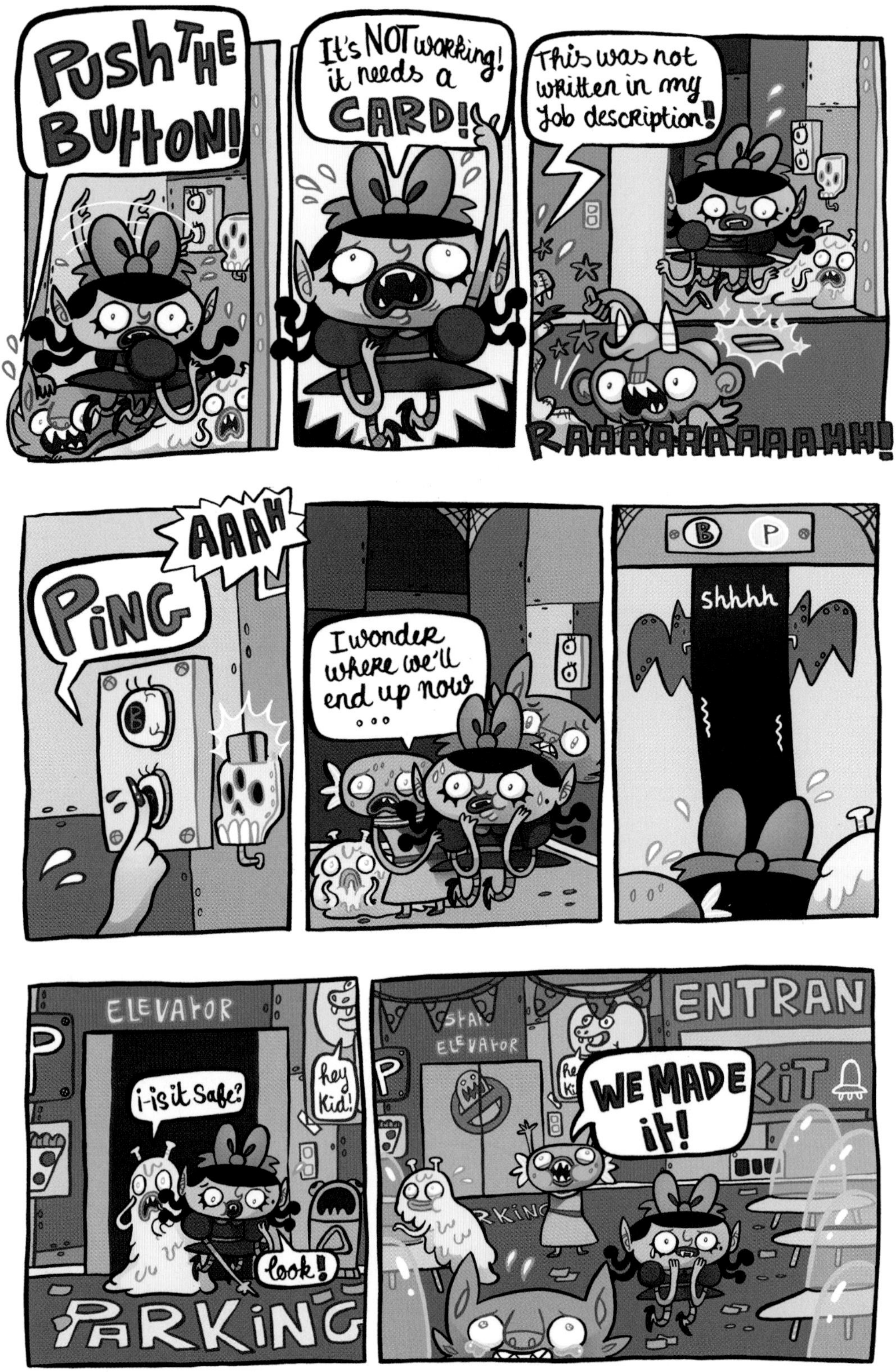

PUSH THE BUTTON!
It's NOT working! it needs a CARD!
This was not written in my Job description!
RAAAAAAAAAAAHH!
PING
AAAH
B
I wonder where we'll end up now ...
B P
shhhh
ELEVATOR
P
i-is it Safe?
hey Kid!
look!
PARKING
ENTRAN
STAFF ELEVATOR
P
WE MADE it!
KiT
RKING

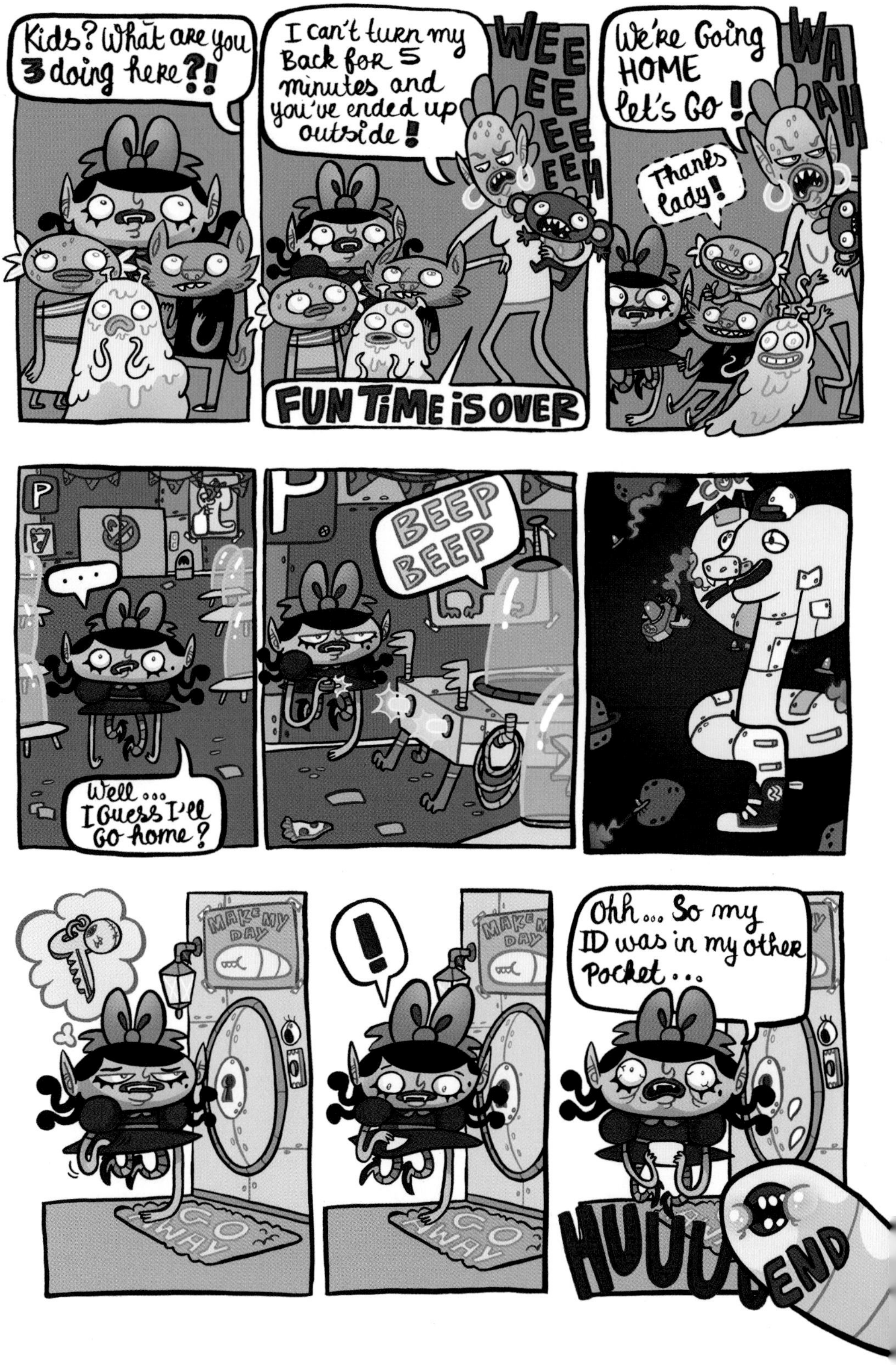
Kids? What are you 3 doing here?!
I can't turn my Back for 5 minutes and you've ended up outside!
WEEEEEEEEH
FUN TIME IS OVER
We're Going HOME let's Go!
WAAAH
Thanks lady!
BEEP BEEP
Well... I Guess I'll Go home?
MAKE MY DAY
GO AWAY
MAKE MY DAY
GO AWAY
!
Ohh... So my ID was in my other Pocket...
HUUU
END

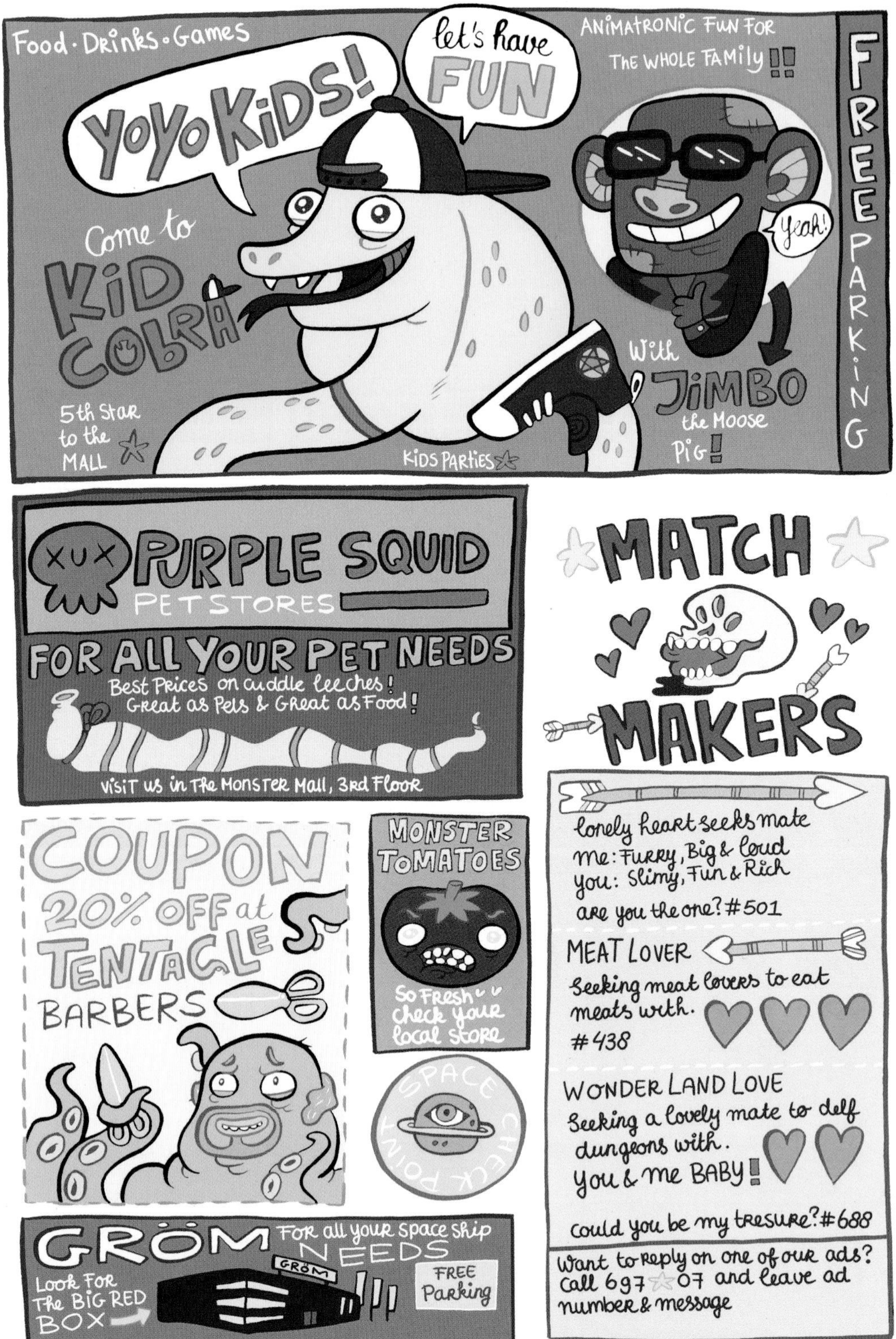
Food • Drinks • Games
YoYo KiDS!
let's have FUN
ANIMATRONIC FUN FOR THE WHOLE FAMily!!
FREE PARKiNG
Come to KiD COBRA
Yeah!
With JiMBO the Moose Pig!
5th Star to the MALL
KiDS PARTiES
PURPLE SQUID PETSTORES
FOR ALL YOUR PET NEEDS
Best Prices on cuddle leeches!
Great as Pets & Great as Food!
ViSiT US iN THE MONSTER MAll, 3Rd Floor
MATCH MAKERS
lonely heart seeks mate
me: Furry, Big & loud
you: Slimy, Fun & Rich
are you the one? #501
MEAT LOVER
Seeking meat lovers to eat meats with.
#438
WONDER LAND LOVE
Seeking a lovely mate to delf dungeons with.
You & me BABY!
could you be my tresure? #688
Want to reply on one of our ads? Call 697☆07 and leave ad number & message
COUPON
20% OFF at TENTACLE BARBERS
MONSTER TOMATOES
So Fresh check your local store
SPACE CHECK POINT
GRÖM
For all your space ship NEEDS
Look For The BIG RED BOX
GRÖM
FREE Parking

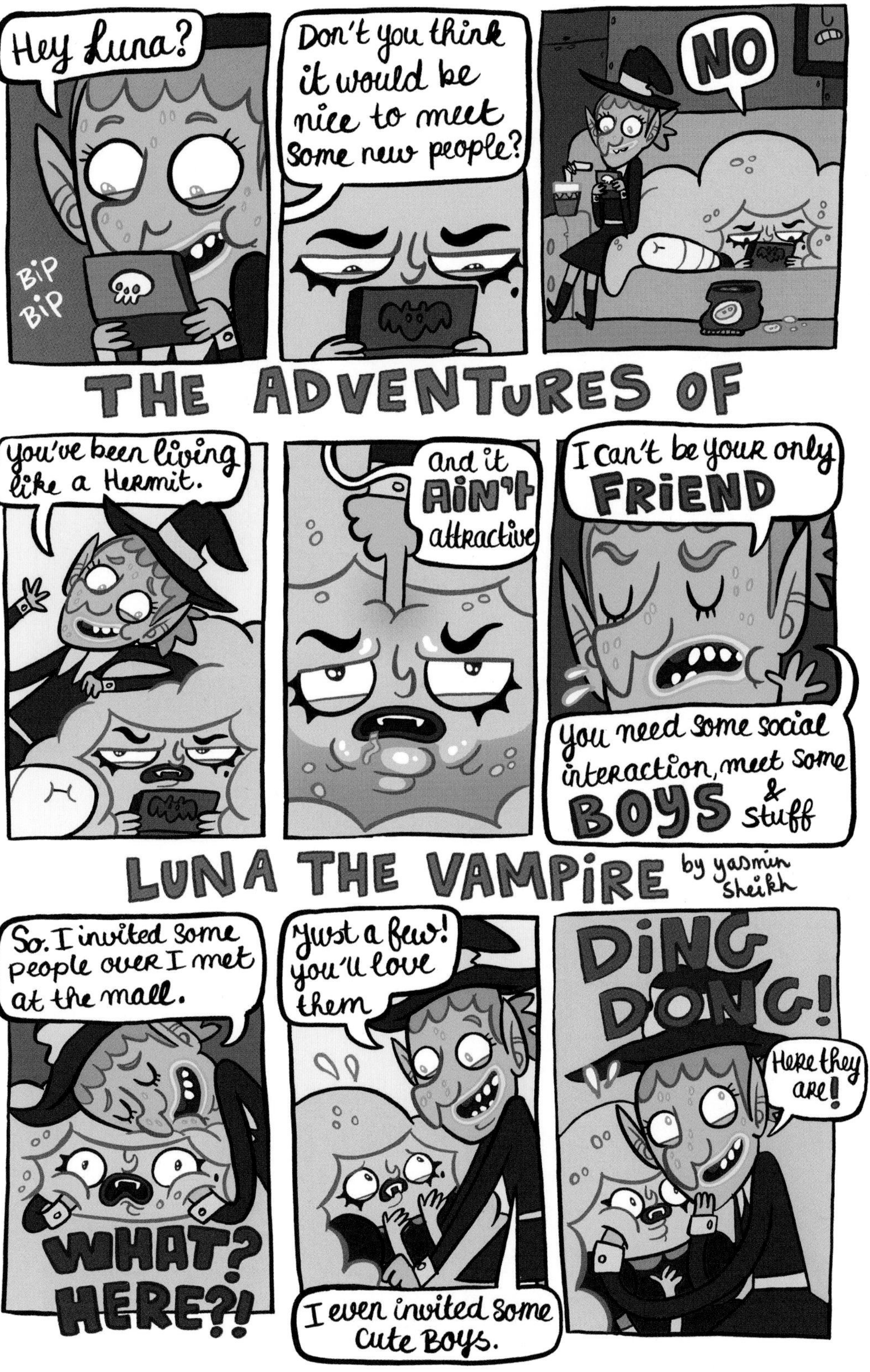
Hey Luna?
BIP BIP
Don't you think it would be nice to meet some new people?
NO
THE ADVENTURES OF
you've been living like a Hermit.
and it AIN'T attractive
I can't be your only FRIEND
You need some social interaction, meet some BOYS & stuff
LUNA THE VAMPIRE
by yasmin sheikh
So. I invited some people over I met at the mall.
WHAT? HERE?!
Just a few! you'll love them
I even invited some Cute Boys.
DING DONG!
Here they are!

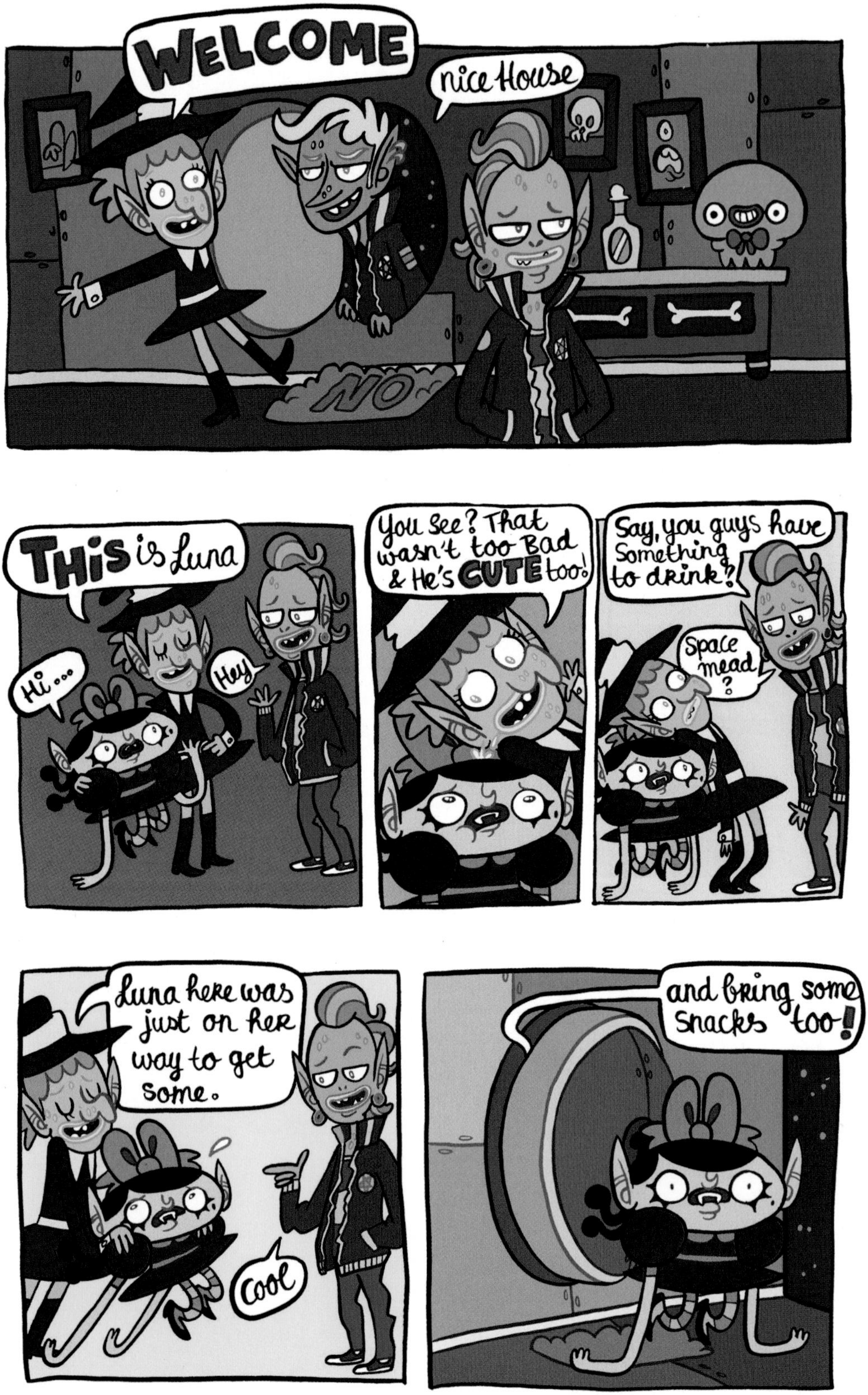
WELCOME
nice House
NO
THIS is Luna
Hi...
Hey
You see? That wasn't too Bad & He's CUTE too!
Say, you guys have Something to drink?
Space mead?
Luna here was just on her way to get some.
Cool
and bring some Snacks too!

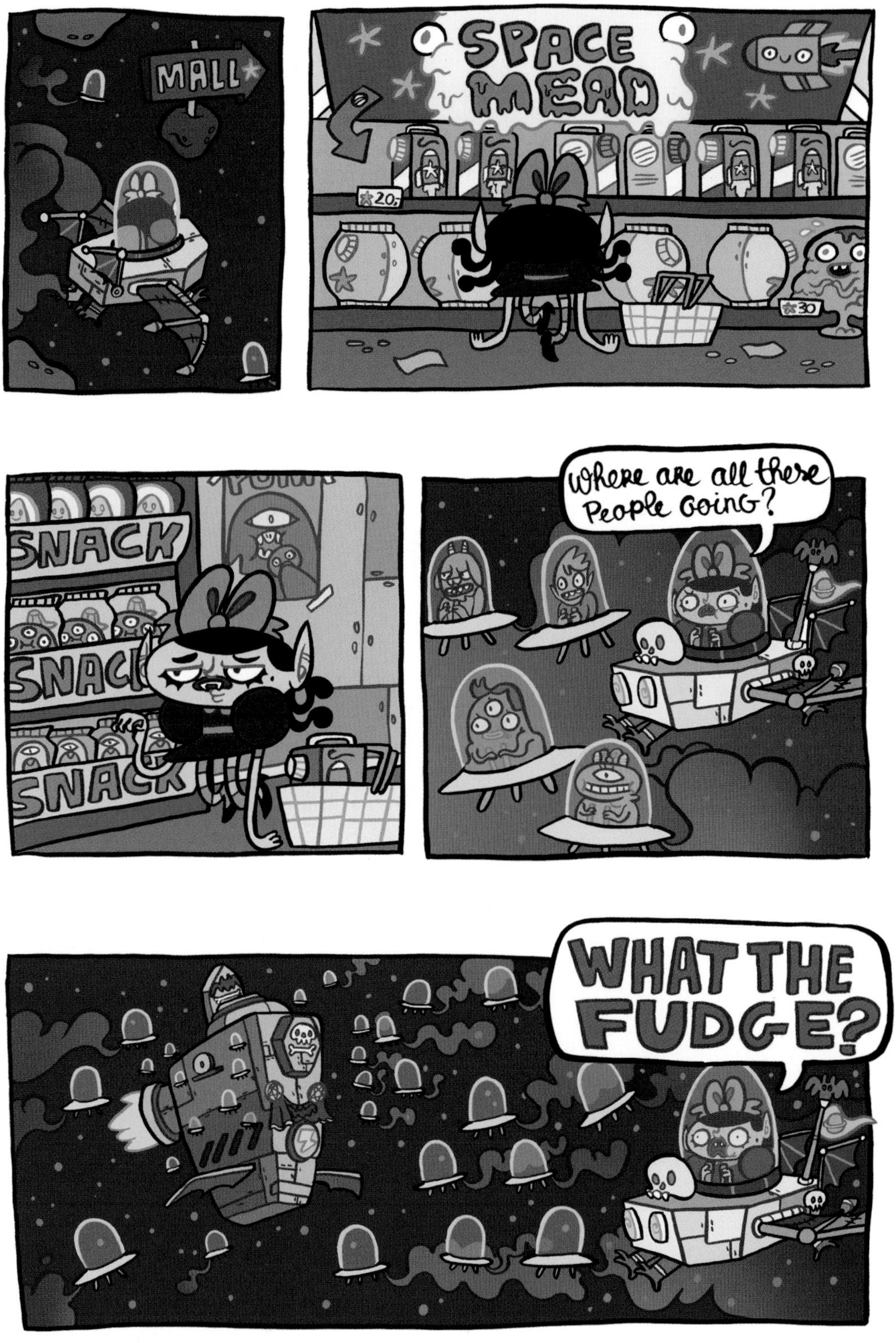
MALL
SPACE MEAD
SNACK
SNACK
SNACK
Where are all these People Going?
WHAT THE FUDGE?

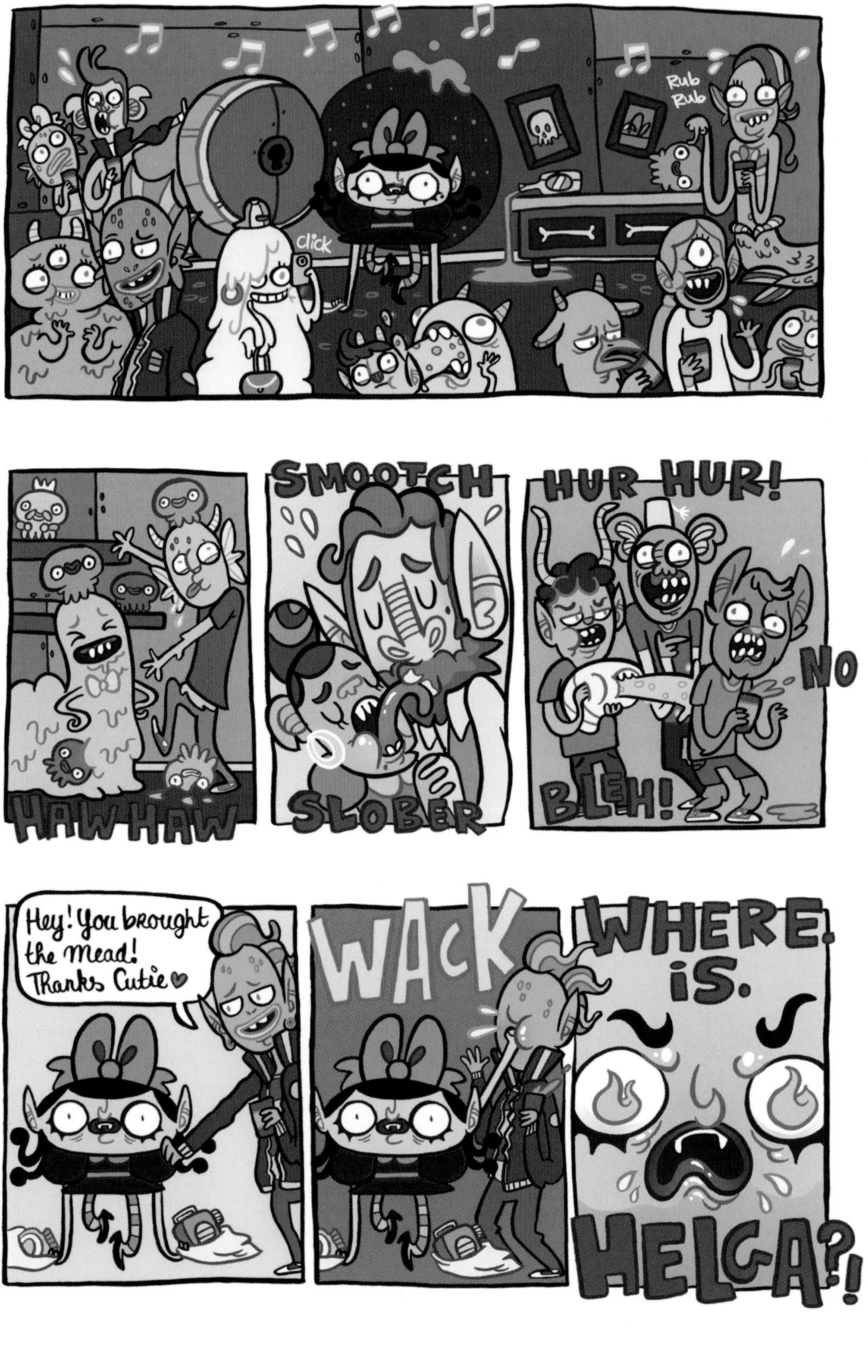
Rub
Rub
click
HAWHAW
SMOOTCH
SLOBER
HUR HUR!
NO
BLEH!
Hey! You brought the Mead! Thanks Cutie
WACK
WHERE.
IS.
HELGA?!

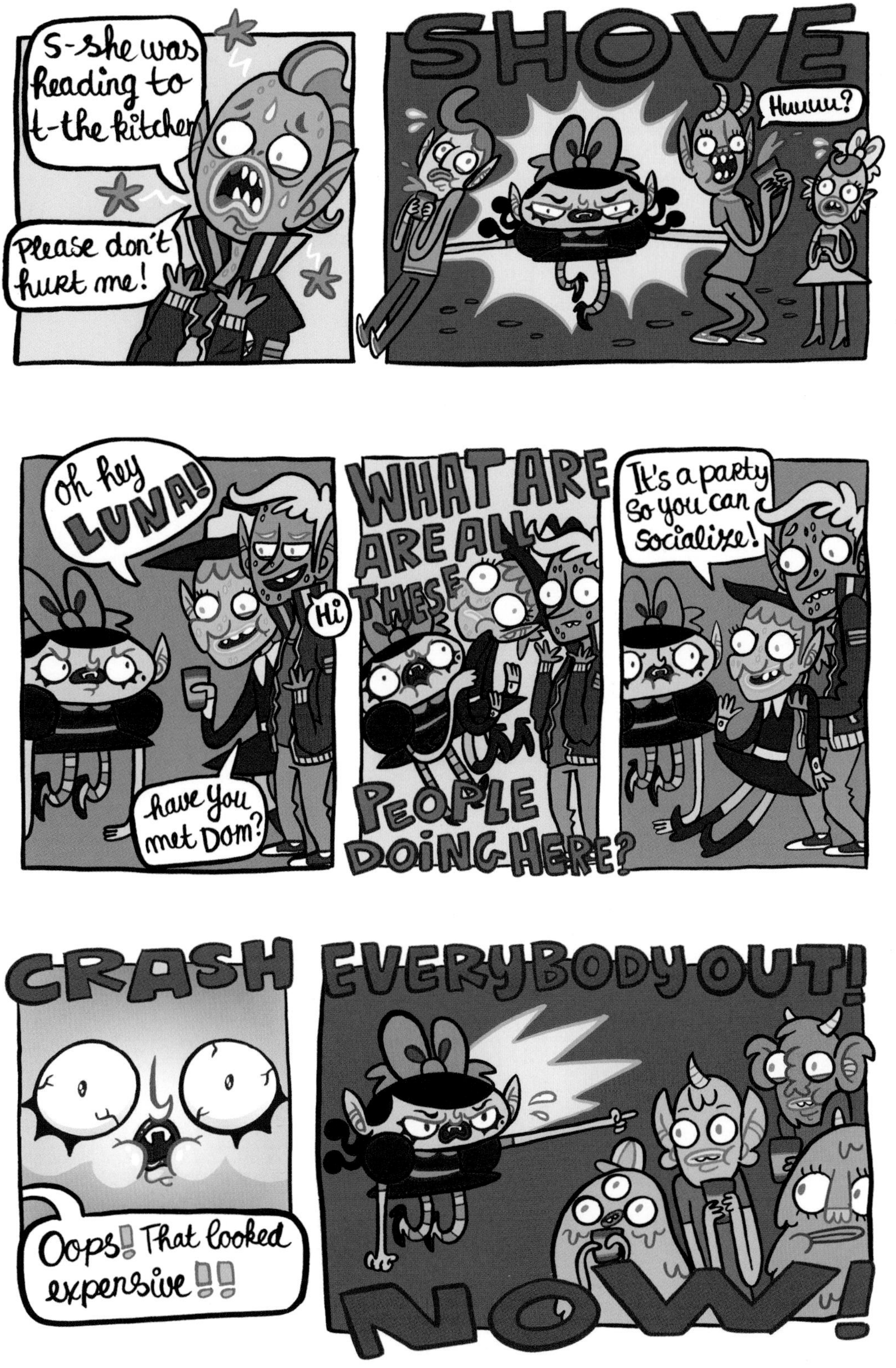
S-she was heading to t-the kitchen
Please don't hurt me!
SHOVE
Huuuu?
Oh hey LUNA!
Hi
have you met Dom?
WHAT ARE ARE ALL THESE PEOPLE DOING HERE?
It's a party so you can socialize!
CRASH
Oops! That looked expensive!!
EVERYBODY OUT! NOW!

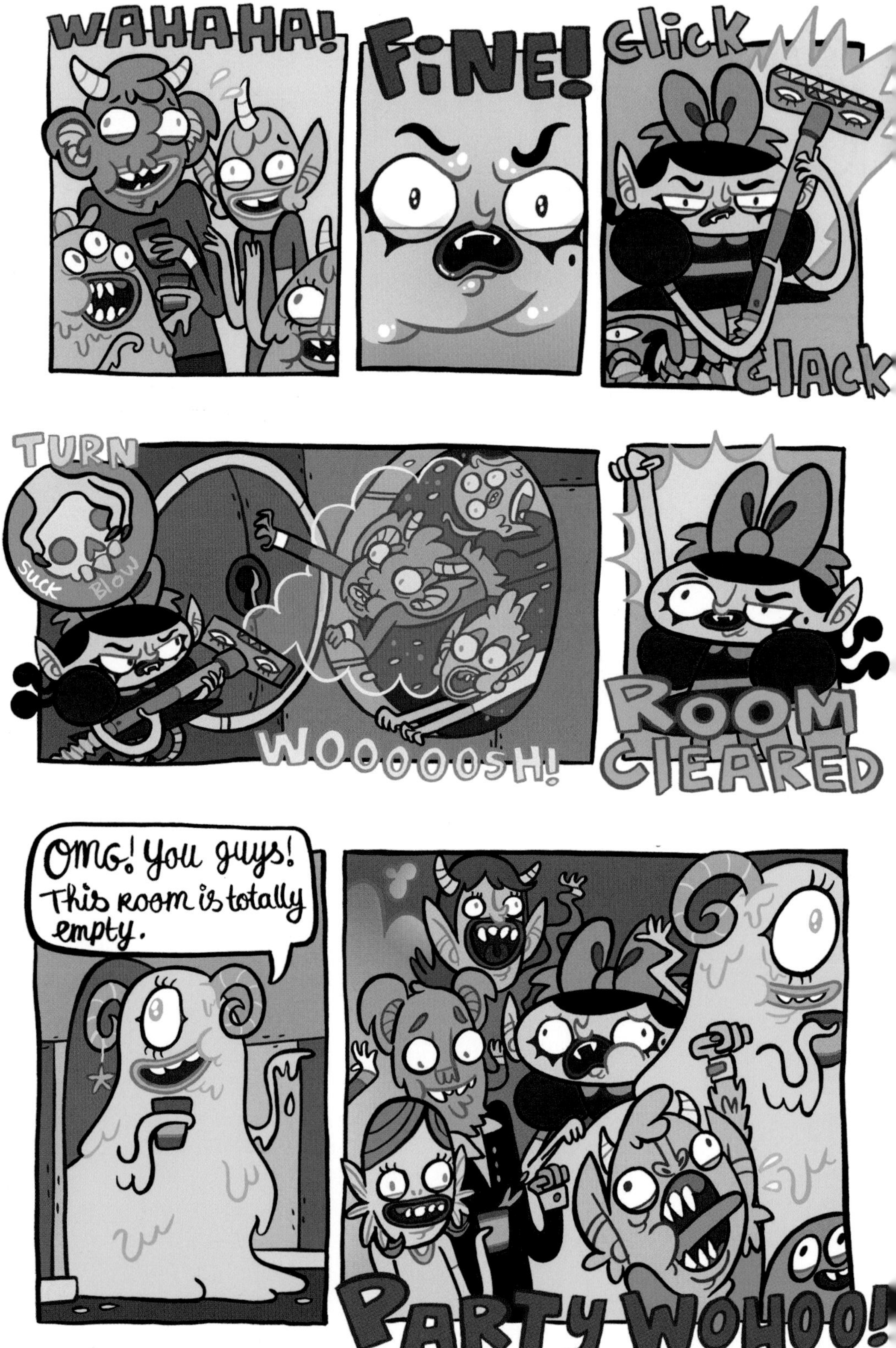
WAHAHA!
FINE!
Click
CLACK
TURN
SUCK
BLOW
WOOOOOOSH!
ROOM CLEARED
OMG! You guys! This room is totally empty.
PARTY WOHOO!

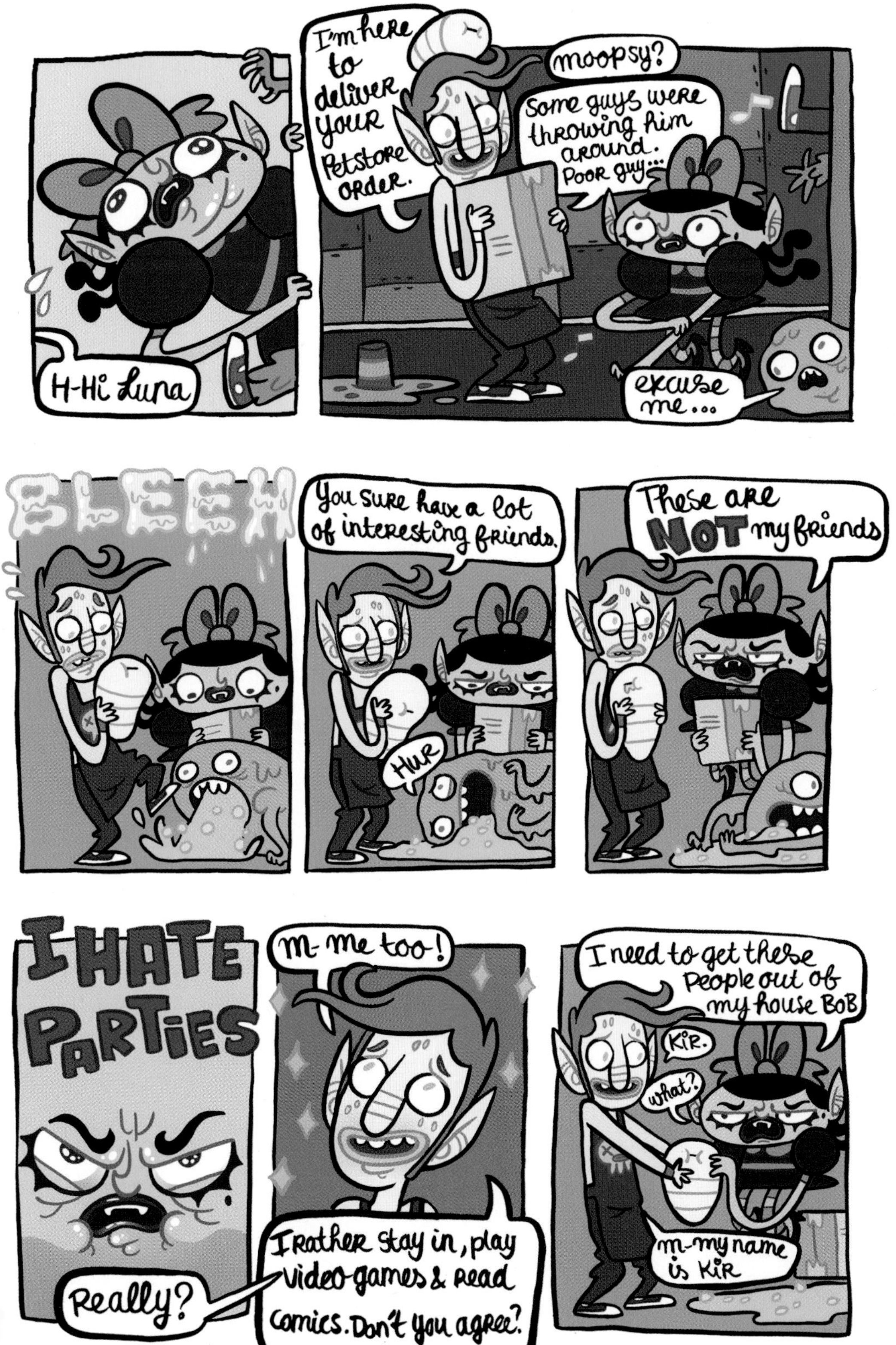
H-Hi Luna
I'm here to deliver your Petstore order.
moopsy?
Some guys were throwing him around. Poor guy...
excuse me...
BLEEH
You sure have a lot of interesting friends.
HUR
These are NOT my friends
I HATE PARTIES
Really?
m-me too!
I rather stay in, play video-games & read comics. Don't you agree?
I need to get these people out of my house BOB
KIR.
what?
m-my name is KIR

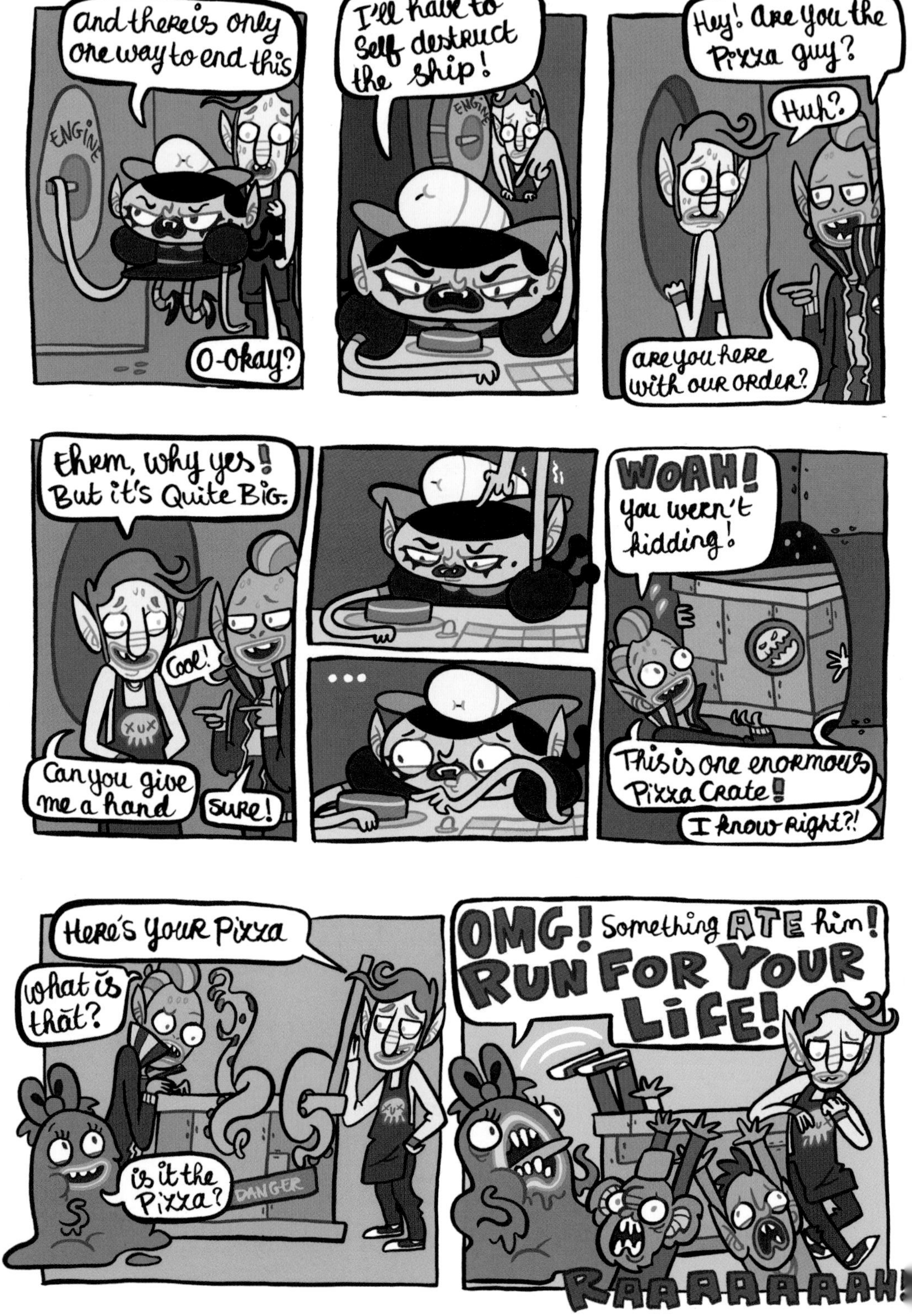

and there is only one way to end this
O-Okay?
I'll have to self destruct the ship!
Hey! Are you the Pizza guy?
Huh?
are you here with our order?
Ehrm, why yes! But it's Quite Big.
Cool!
Can you give me a hand
Sure!
WOAH! you weren't kidding!
This is one enormous Pizza Crate!
I know right?!
Here's your Pizza
what is that?
is it the Pizza?
DANGER
OMG! Something ATE him! RUN FOR YOUR LIFE!
RAAAAAAAAH!

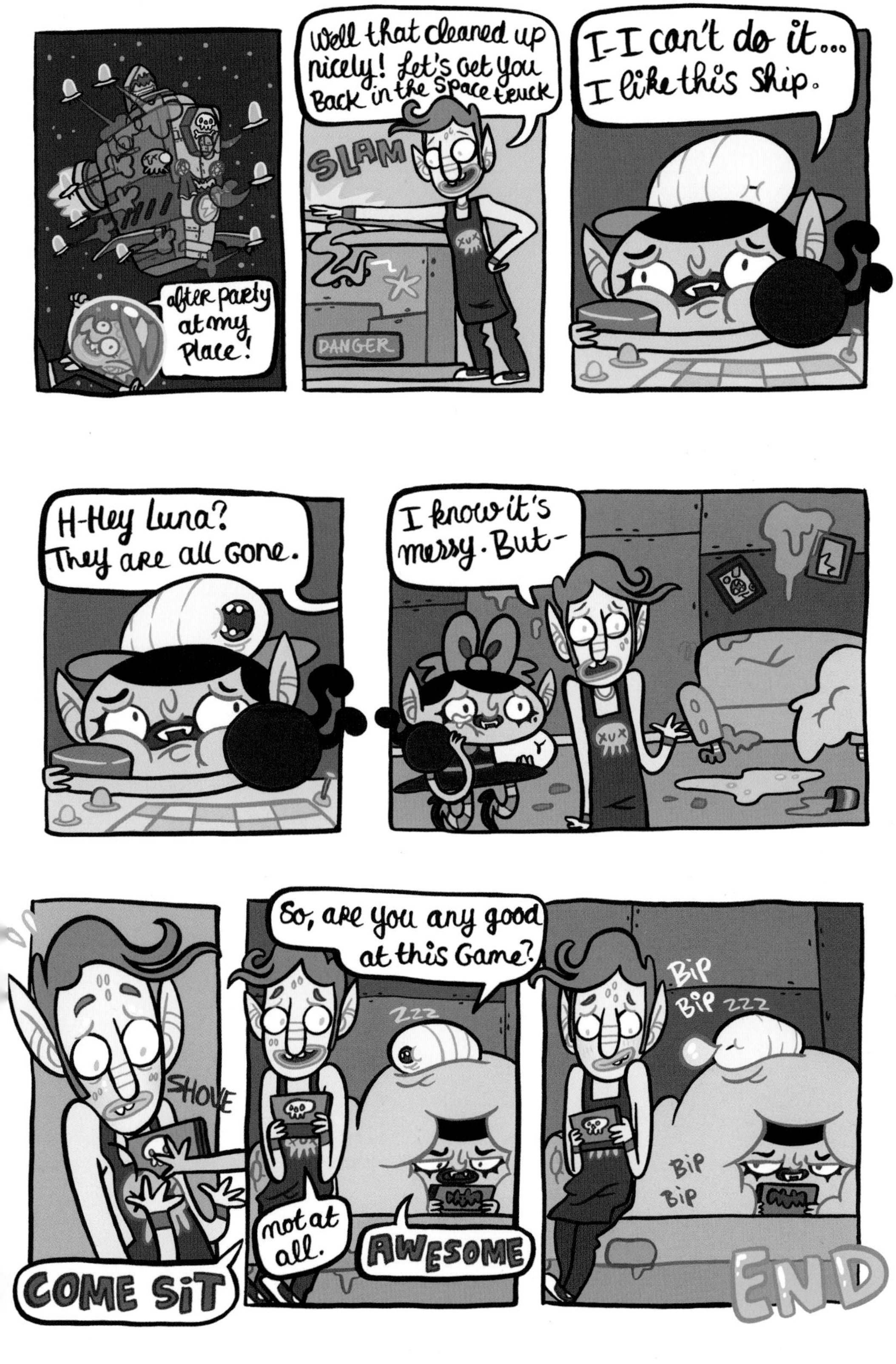
after party at my Place!
Well that cleaned up nicely! Let's get you Back in the Space truck
SLAM
DANGER
I-I can't do it... I like this Ship.
H-Hey Luna? They are all Gone.
I know it's messy. But-
COME SIT
SHOVE
So, are you any good at this Game?
not at all.
AWESOME
ZZZ
BIP BIP ZZZ
BIP BIP
END

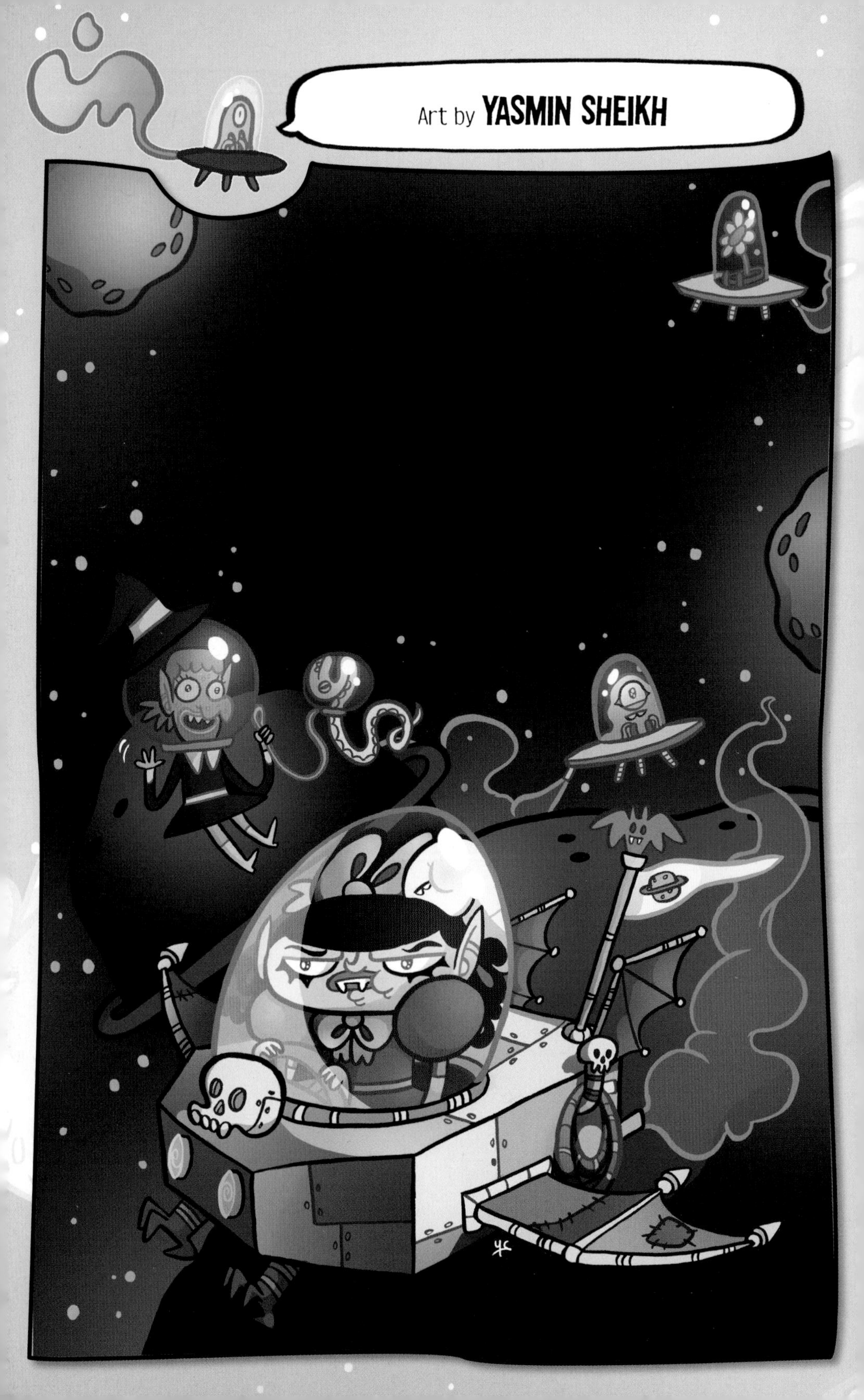
Art by YASMIN SHEIKH

Art by **AMY MEBBERSON**

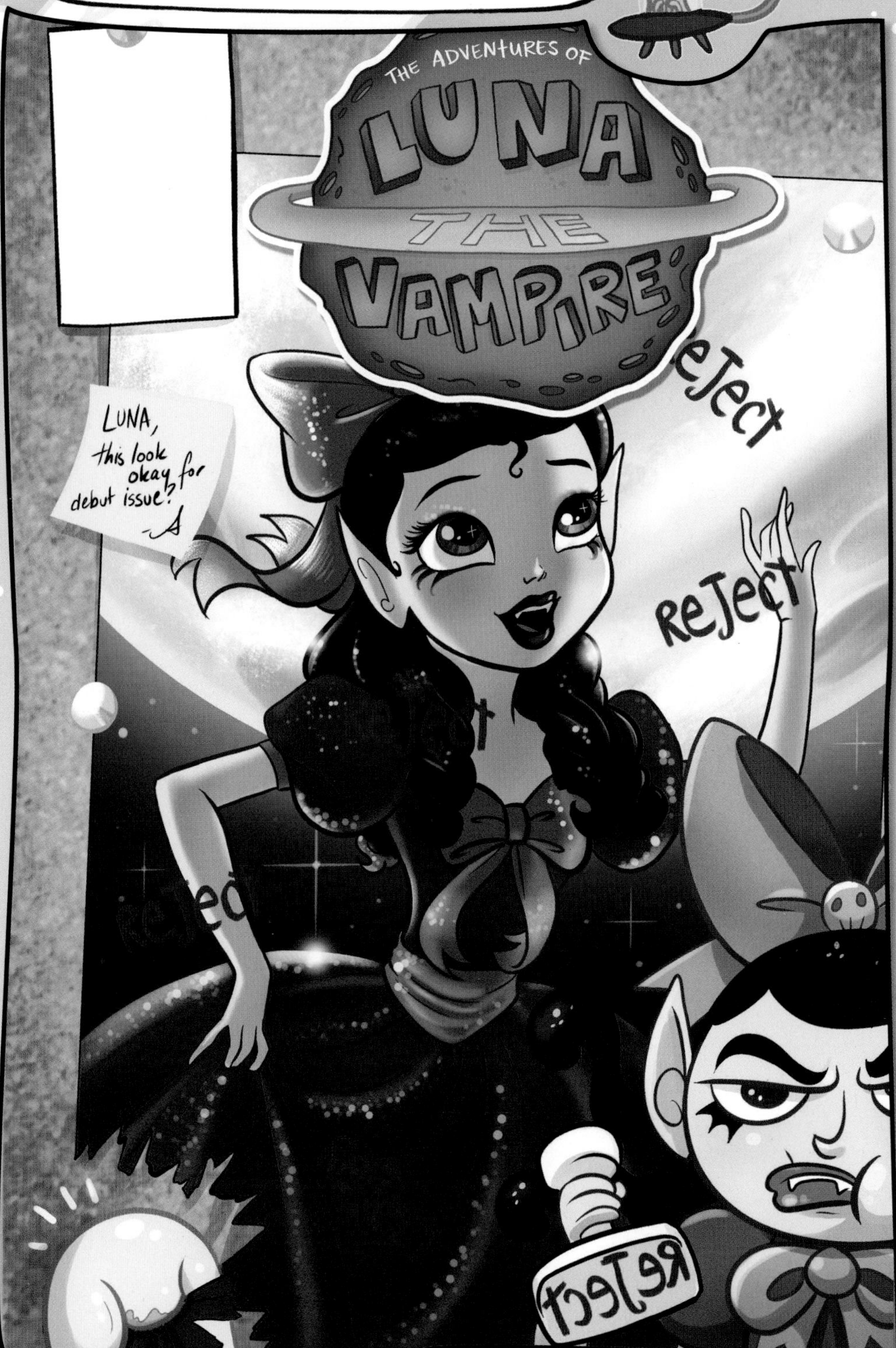

THE ADVENTURES OF
LUNA
THE
VAMPIRE
LUNA, this look okay for debut issue? -A
reJect
ReJect
ReJect

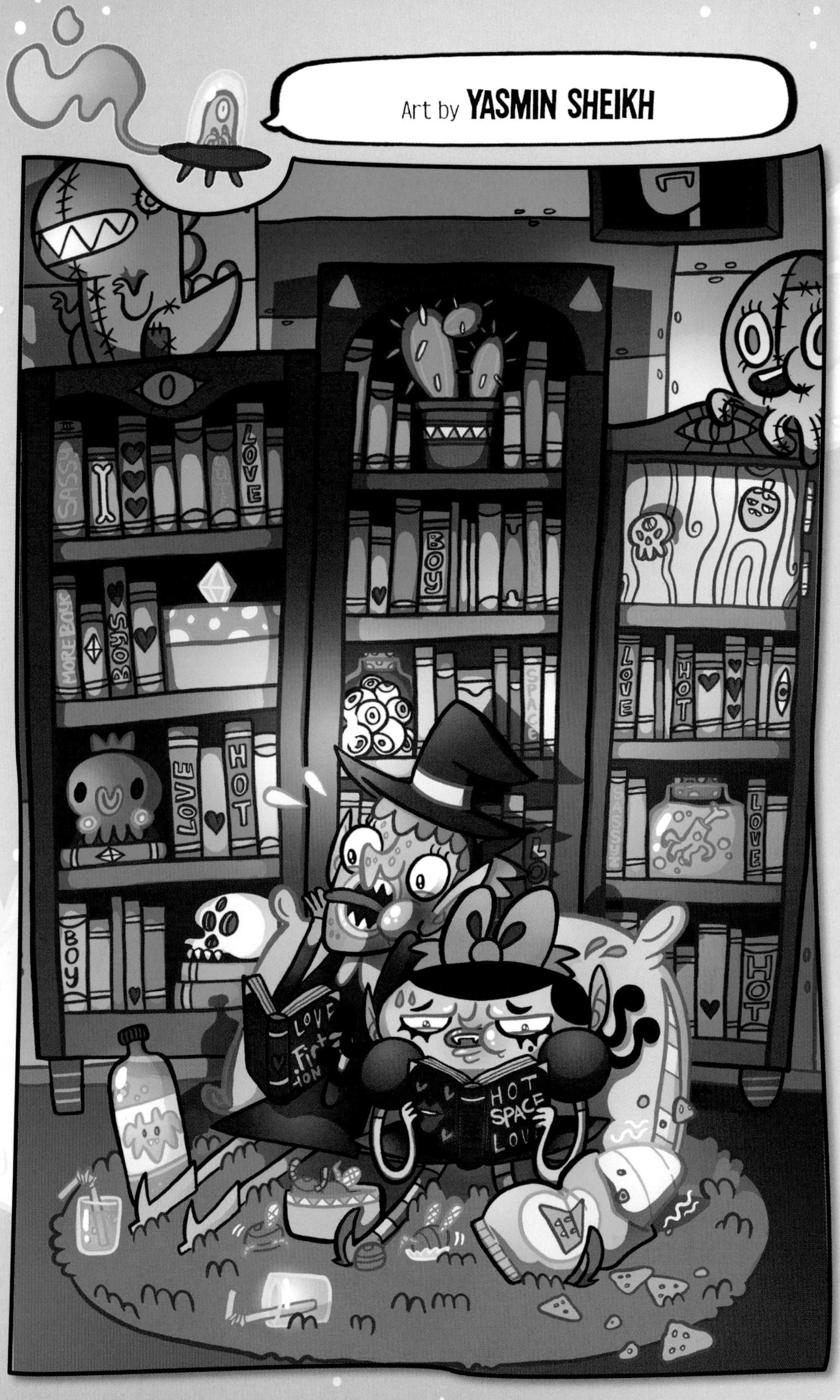
Art by YASMIN SHEIKH
SASSY
LOVE
MORE BOYS
BOYS
LOVE
HOT
BOY
SPACE
LOVE
HOT
LOVE
BOY
HOT
LOVE Fiction
HOT SPACE LOVE

Art by **TOM JILESEN**

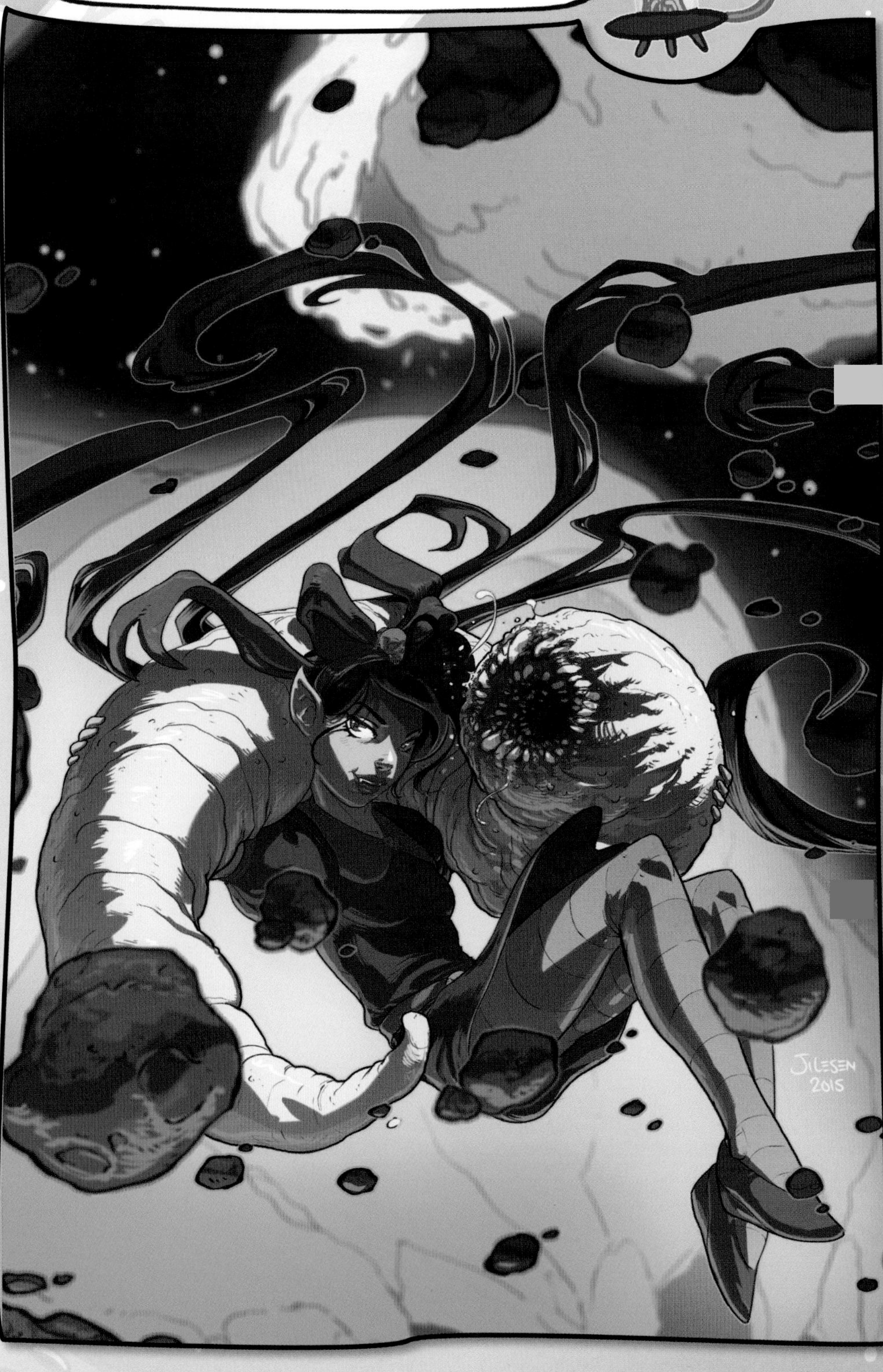
JILESEN
2015

Art by **YASMIN SHEIKH**

TO:_____

FROM:_____

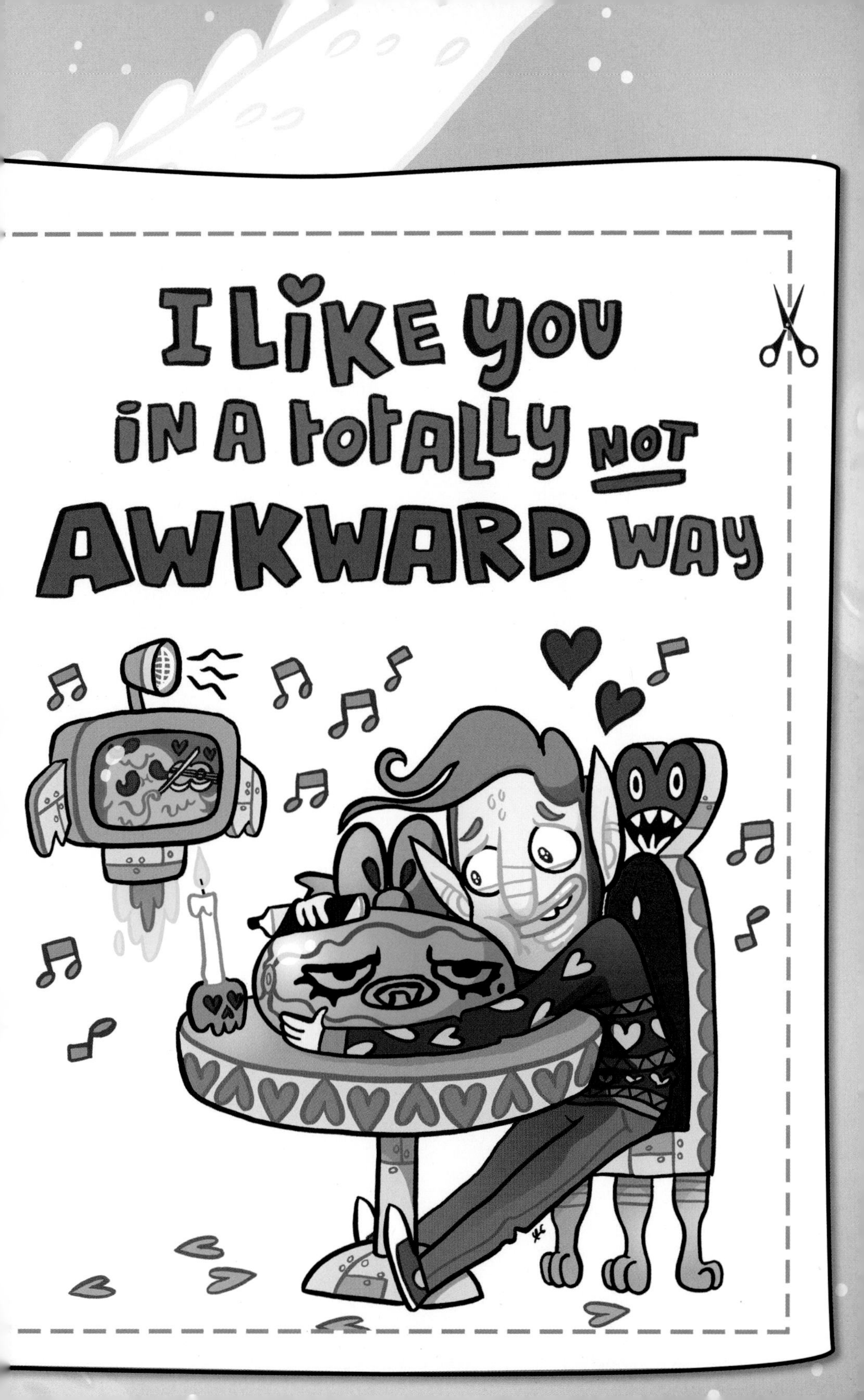
I LIKE YOU
IN A TOTALLY NOT
AWKWARD WAY

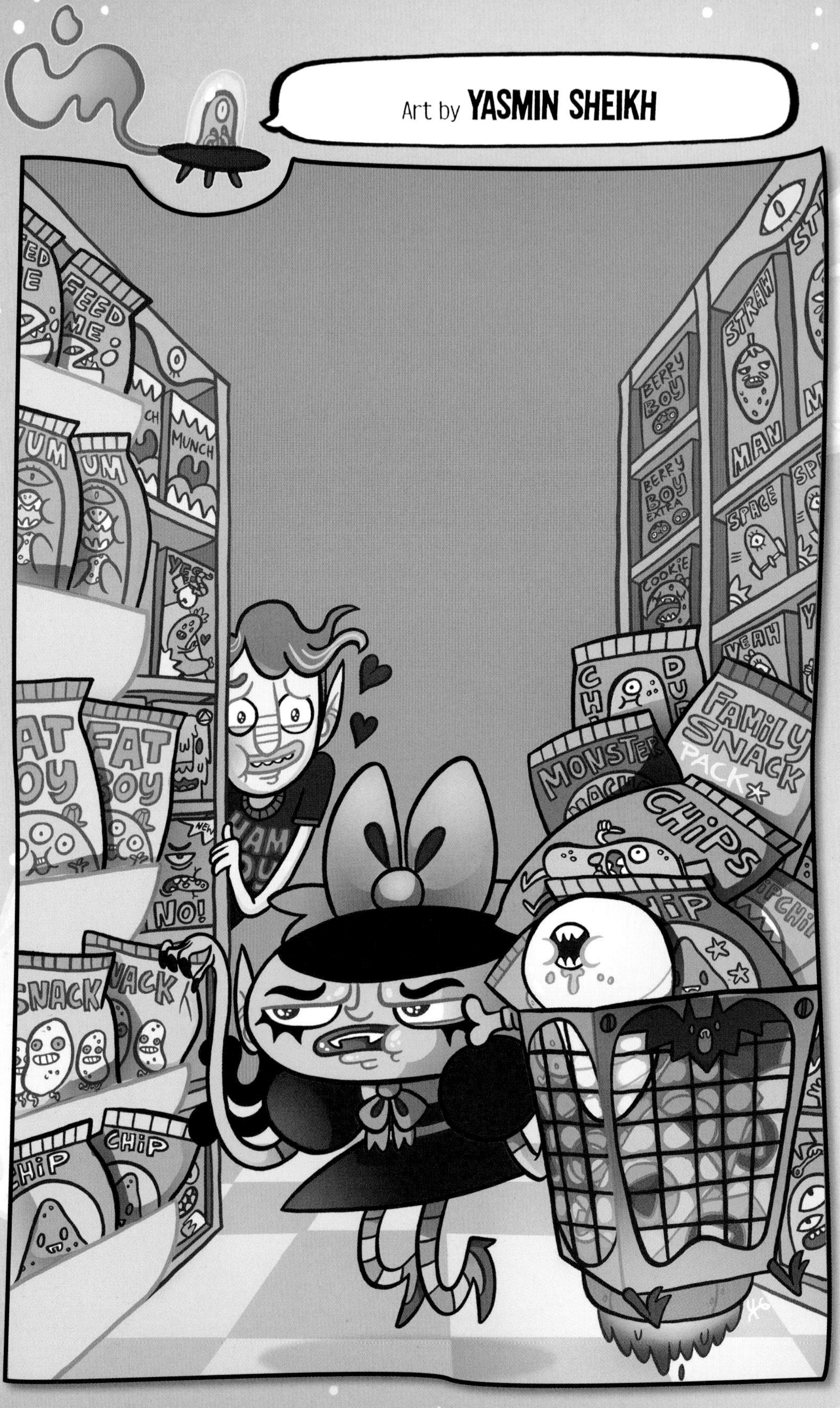
Art by YASMIN SHEIKH
FEED ME
YUM
MUNCH
FAT BOY
NO!
SNACK
CHIP
BERRY BOY
BERRY BOY EXTRA
STRAW MAN
SPACE
COOKIE
YEAH
MONSTER
FAMILY SNACK PACK
CHIPS

Art by **ROBIN KEIJZER**

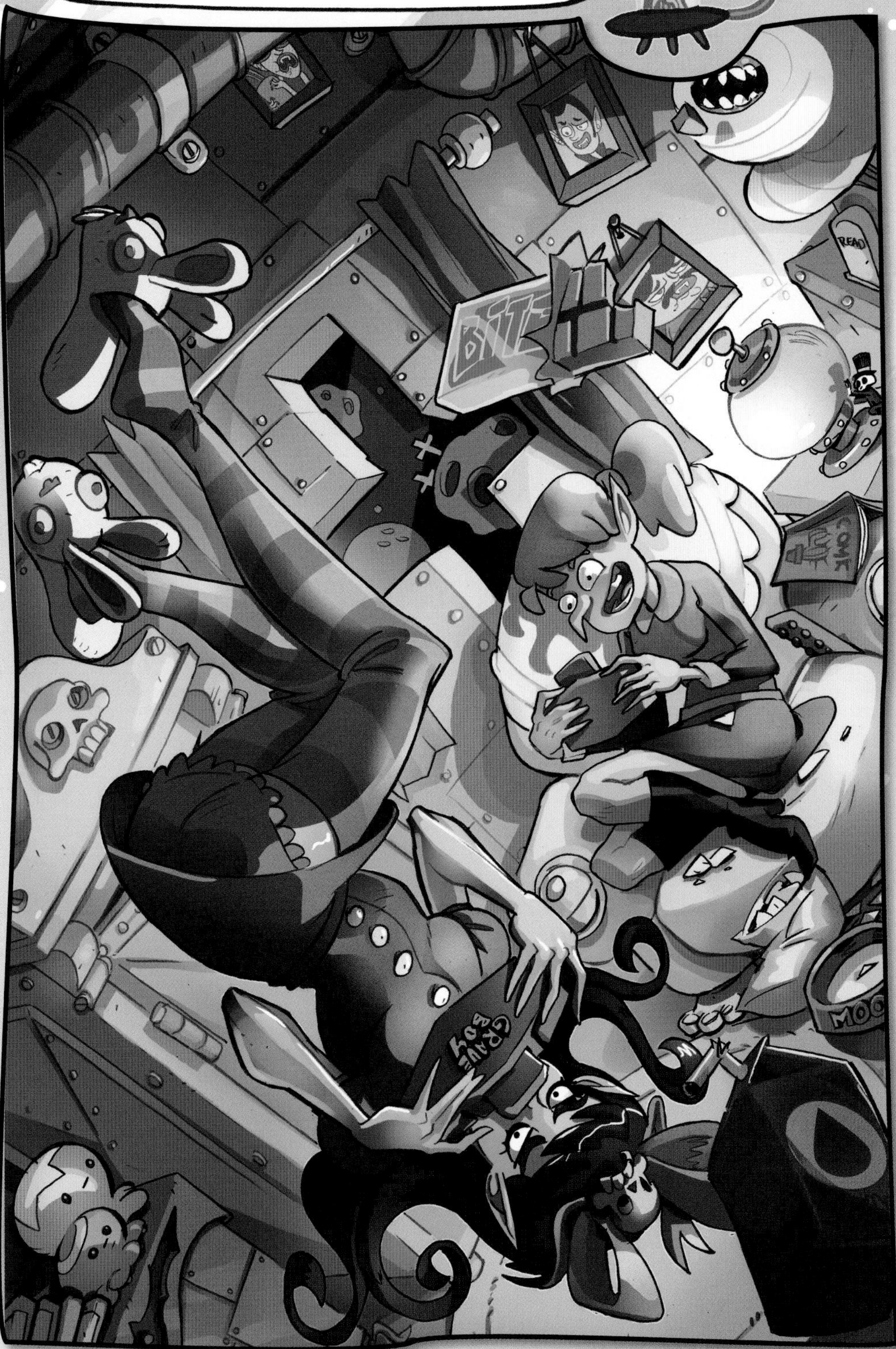
READ

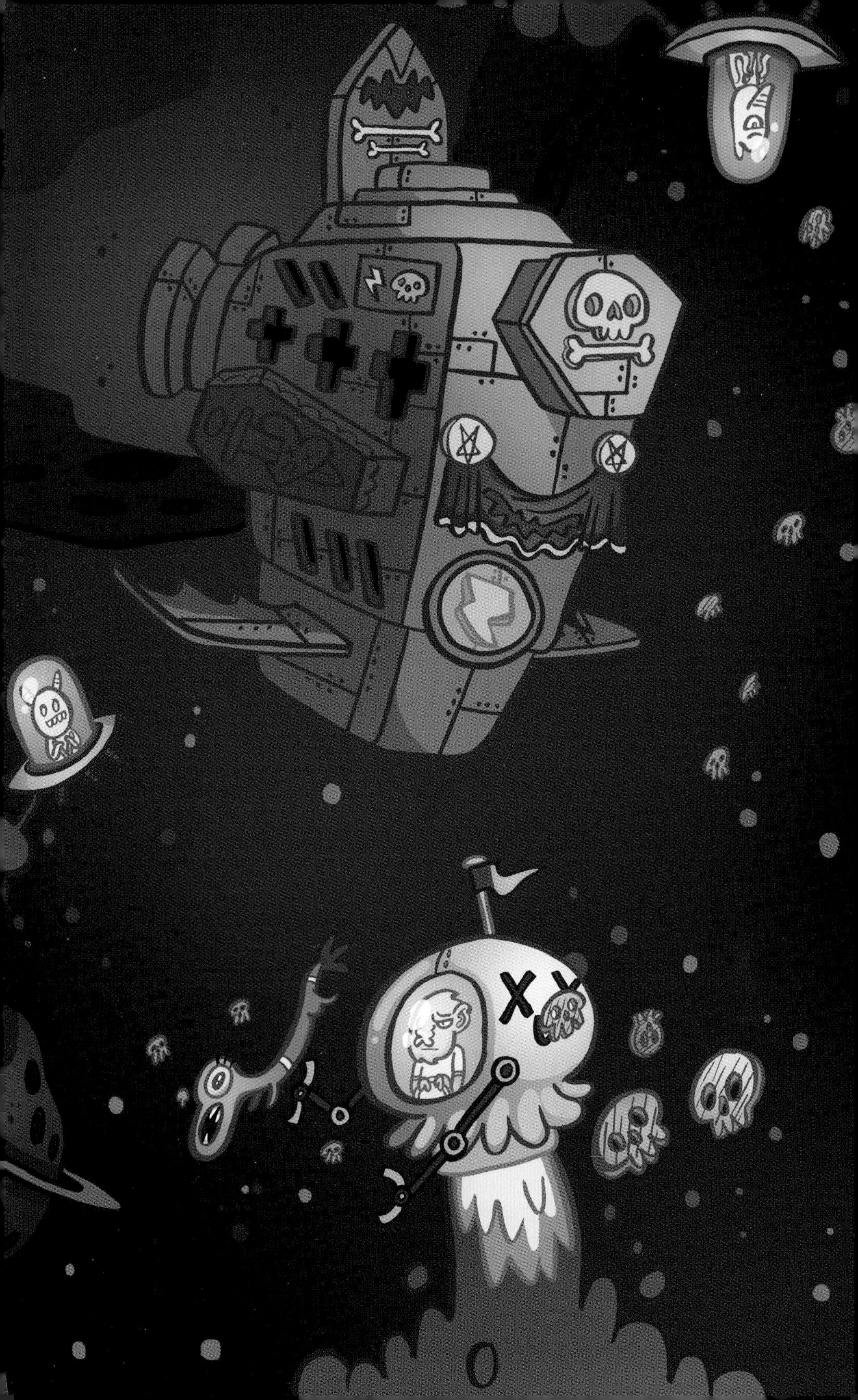